S0-BRJ-851

INTERIOR DESIGN
and *Other*
Emotions

INTERIOR DESIGN AND OTHER EMOTIONS

Copyright © 2016 by Kate Forest
Sale of the electronic edition of this book is wholly unauthorized.
Except for use in review, the reproduction or utilization of this
work in whole or in part, by any means, is forbidden without
written permission from the author/publisher.
Kate Forest, publisher
This book is a work of fiction. Names, characters, places, and
incidents are products of the author's imagination or are used
fictitiously. Any resemblance to actual events, locales, or persons,
living or dead, is entirely coincidental.
All rights reserved, including the right to reproduce this book or
portions thereof in any form whatsoever.

To Pam

INTERIOR DESIGN
and Other
Emotions

KATE FOREST

Happy Ever After

Kate Forest

To everyone who struggles to find love and meaning.
Which means all of us.

Chapter 1

CHRISTOPHER

"Double-shot caramel mochaccino."

The barista places the tan travel mug on the counter. It's that weird barista who looks familiar. I don't dwell on where I might know her because I'm thrown off by her actions, like she's a robot trying to function in a world of humans. She always smiles in the strangest way, like she's waiting for me to say something back. I grab my drink and duck out of the shop with the briefest of nods. The last thing I want is to get into a conversation with someone who can't hold a real job.

The temperature is already too high for a Monday morning. I should've gotten an iced coffee, but those are for pussies. Drinking coffee from a straw? Please.

The leather soles of my Prada bluchers clack against the metal door to the storage cellar of the Korean market I pass by every day on my way to the glorious skyscraper where I work. I'll be two minutes late for the morning meeting.

Exactly what I planned.

Showing up early for work on a Monday means you care too much. Timing it perfectly is key to letting everyone know you care about the job, but you're no slave.

Extracting myself from the long legs of the blonde this morning wasn't easy. Plus, she lives out in Brooklyn Heights. I had to get up with the newspaper delivery truck to haul ass to my place to shower and change. She wasn't a natural blonde anyway. I discovered that in the cab ride from the club.

As soon as I turn onto Beaver Street, I smile. It might be juvenile; I also snicker at Rector Street. But once inside the cool marble chrome and overly air-conditioned building where I toil, I put my game face on.

My five-month-old MBA grants me access to this mecca of money, and I take full advantage.

"Hold up." Rob runs toward the closing elevator doors. He's the no-shit-taking, hard-ass trader I hang with.

I smirk and at the last minute put my hand between the doors. A groan comes from the back. I don't turn when someone mumbles something about "already being late."

Rob and I are part of the elite club—we can make the secretaries wait.

"Thanks, dude." Rob nods to the other riders. "How'd it go last night?" He drops his voice and leans into me. After he took off from the club, I'd made my move on the blonde.

"Like you need to ask." I take a sip of my drink. It's warm and sweet. Like the fake blonde. Like the hair dye she used as a disguise, no one would know I drank girl coffee unless they peeked underneath the lid. That's why I buy my coffee from a shop blocks away. From the outside my cup looks like a manly large coffee. Inside, chocolate and whipped cream make the caffeine slide down.

We exit when the doors swoosh open at one of the five floors of the investment and financial analysis firm of Humbolt and Sutter.

"You sure opened your wallet for that dude in the club. You must have spent a few hundred bucks buying him Stoli shots and Cristal for his date." Rob walks with me to my office and stands in the doorway while I drop into my chair.

"He had two dates." I fire up my laptop.

"Who is he? He blackmailing you for something from your past?" Rob chuckles.

"He's an old fraternity buddy. And he probably has enough dirt on me from our wild days. But no, he's just out of a job and I wanted to show him a good time." I don't add that I also sprang for him and his two dates to get a suite in the Millennium. Rob is a great guy, one of the best traders. But he's not the most sophisticated, and I'm sure he's a bigger gossip than my Aunt Sophia.

"Oh yeah. Where did he work?"

"Some pharmaceutical company." I shrug like I don't know and don't care. But I know every detail of his work. At least the parts I can understand without a PhD in biology. "He got laid off and I felt bad for him." *And he had intel to sell.* The drinks and the hotel room were an investment in my career. Because what he shared with me will pay off big time.

"Well, I gotta check in before the opening bell." Rob slaps the doorframe. "Next weekend is going to be awesome."

"You know you've made it when you have a weekend share of a house in the Hamptons."

"The good end of Long Island." Rob follows me into the meeting room.

I might have to pass through my old neighborhood in Queens to get there, but I'll never stop off on my way to a new life.

Chapter 2

GINA

"Double-shot caramel mochaccino with whipped cream," Becky calls.

That drink requires a half-ounce of syrup and two shots of espresso. I fill the twenty-ounce cup to the precise measurements.

I echo the order as I place it on the pick-up counter. I remember to smile, which is done by stretching your cheek and showing a little bit of your teeth. Christopher Rinaldi takes it with a nod. Christopher Rinaldi comes in every day, except he has missed two days of work in the past five months.

He lived at 316 Eighty-Second Avenue in Kew Gardens. Three houses away from me. Until the day after his sister drowned. That was six years, five months, and three days ago.

"Gina, we need more sixteen-ounce cups," Becky says.

"How many?" I ask.

"A ton. Look at this rush. It's Monday morning, you idiot."

I need to use the bathroom, my back has an itch, and my left shoe isn't tied properly. I shift side to side.

"Give her a number. You have to give her a number," Sarah tells Becky, and smiles at me.

"Fine. One hundred seventeen." Becky's smile is not soft like Sarah's.

Calm. The itch disappears.

Prime numbers are easy to see.

I retrieve one hundred and seventeen cups from the storeroom, and the rest of the morning proceeds as it usually does. Except that the lady who leaves her pug tied outside to the parking meter takes an especially long time to decide what she wants. Instead of her usual yogurt, she orders a breakfast sandwich. That means the dog is tied to the meter for an extra three minutes and thirty-five seconds.

When people are done with their lunch, I find Sarah to remind her of my schedule.

"Monday afternoons at two p.m. I have —"

"We know, we know. Gina, you don't have to tell us each week." Becky lets out a big breath like she has been running.

"Just go home after your appointment." Sarah is the manager of Perks Plus. It is a coffee shop that also sells pastries and sandwiches. That is the plus.

"I'll meet my grandmother at the Center for Autism Services, and then I'm supposed to come back to finish my shift."

"Take the afternoon off. You put in enough hours last week." Sarah nods.

"I worked an extra five and a half hours last week."

"Then it's only fair if you go home and let Becky have the extra hours."

"Okay." I remove my apron and take my MetroCard out of its plastic holder.

"We've got to get you a decent purse." Sarah watches me as I get ready to leave.

"My nonna gave me this purse. We bought it at the discount store. It matches my skirt for church."

"I'm sure it does..." Sarah stops talking and scrunches her facial features.

People do that a lot. They start to say something and then forget what they were going to say. Nonna calls it "finding the right words." As if words need to be found. How can people forget words? But I wait, even though the itch on my back is starting. I need to leave soon so I won't be late.

"Never mind." Sarah waves her hand. "Forget I said anything."

"Okay." I turn to leave. But how can I forget that she spoke? And why would I want to forget? People should say what they mean.

The bus ride takes twenty-three minutes. Nonna waits outside.

"Gina, how was work?" She rubs my back right where I get itches. It feels good.

"Christopher Rinaldi ordered a double-shot mochaccino, and we ran out of sesame bagels at eight thirty."

Nonna stops walking right when we get inside the building. I halt and wait for her.

"Chris Rinaldi came into the coffee shop?"

"He does every morning between eight forty-five and eight fifty. He lived three houses down from me when I lived with Mom and Dad. His sister — "

"Hurry, Regina, we'll be late." Nonna takes my elbow and guides me to the room where I meet with my social worker, Jennifer.

Jennifer greets us, and we sit in the yellow room. It has lemon-yellow walls and the chairs are more canary yellow. The carpet is mostly a coffee brown with banana stripes. There are minimal accent pieces. A framed print of a 1997 Picasso exhibit is the only decoration.

The furniture is arranged in a square, which doesn't make the best use of the space. There are many square feet lost by this placement. I have tried to explain this to Jennifer, and she says it has to be this way.

"Gina, your grandmother and I have been talking about a new study we think would be good for you to take part in."

"Okay."

"It means taking medicine every day. The medicine might help you learn more of the emotions we work to understand. And everyone in the Thursday support group will take the medicine, and we can all talk about how the medicine makes us feel."

"Jennifer, you're taking the medicine, too? I don't think you should. You do not have autism, and I think you already know all the emotions you need to know. Taking medication that you don't need can be dangerous. Over two million people go to the emergency room each year for misusing prescription drugs."

"Yes, sorry, Gina." Jennifer laughs, and I return the laugh with the chuckle we practiced. It's done by forcing bursts of air through the throat. "So, you're okay with taking a new medicine?"

"Can I read the drug fact sheet?"

"Of course. It's for all sorts of people on the spectrum. People who would have had an Asperger's diagnosis like you a few years ago, and anyone else who comes here for help." Jennifer hands me the paper with the formulation and contraindications listed. I read the information while Nonna and Jennifer talk.

"It says it's a double-blind study. I might get a placebo."

Jennifer nods. "Yes, a placebo is —"

"I know what it is. What if I don't get the medicine?"

"That's the way a study works. There's a risk

9

you'll just be taking sugar pills."

I know there's no risk in taking a placebo. Nothing can happen to you if you do, and maybe I will get the medicine.

I sign all the papers Jennifer gives me after reading each one. It explains how all patients will take part in the study, Level One, like me, and Two and Three. Nonna signs too. She has been my custodian ever since I went to live with her, which was five years, ten months, and seven days ago.

"Nonna, I can go home with you. Sarah said my shift was over for the day."

"Okay, *cara*."

We take the R train to Rego Park. Nonna has lived in her narrow house since before I was born, twenty-four years, three months, and two days ago.

"Look, Gina, new catalogues." Nonna takes the mail out of the white box attached to the doorframe. It's held there by six Phillips-head screws.

My heart races. New catalogues mean new room arrangements. Pottery Barn always uses the same accent pieces, and so I head to the storage room. Nonna lets me keep all of my surplus in the room that used to be my mother's bedroom. She slept on the first floor in the back. Her siblings all shared bedrooms upstairs.

"I think I'll re-create this one." I point to a picture of a country living room with paneled walls and clean white lines.

"That will be lovely. And we can go to all the yard sales this weekend. I bet we can find something similar to those paintings." She points to the artwork on the walls of the staged room.

"Uh-huh." I start by picking up the coffee table and carrying it into the storage room.

CHRISTOPHER

"I've got the order ready to go. All I need from you is your go-ahead," Rob says into his headset. "It comes down to this, Mr. Glass. Do you want to play it safe or take this risk? Because it is a risk. The market offers no guarantees, but the rewards can be worth it..."

I roll my eyes and wait for him to finish his pitch. I need to make sure he understands the analysis before I can leave for the day.

"Mr. Glass, let me congratulate you." Rob hits a few keys on his keyboard. "You can log in and check the action in your account any time."

"I can't believe they fall for your bullshit." I lean against the wall of his cubicle.

"People believe what they want to. He wanted to risk his retirement on this IPO before he even called me. I just helped him do it."

"What's the company, anyway?"

Rob shrugs. "Doesn't matter. We're bundling it all together with a bunch of companies that never got enough capital. To the retail investor it looks like they're getting in on the ground floor, when really the fate of these start-ups has already been decided. And they're not going anywhere."

"Did you get my report?"

I kick his chair, and he wheels to the end of his desk.

"Yeah. Buy low, sell high."

"Rob, there's intel from a pharma company that—" My phone vibrates and the screen reads "family." Momma has called three times today. I've ignored each one. "Shit. I'll be back." I turn from Rob and stalk out to the hall.

"Momma?" I answer.

"Christofo, why didn't you answer me before?"

"I'm at work, Momma. I can't take personal calls. I'm busy." I stride into my tiny office and kick the door closed behind me. It rattles against the glass pane. The bigger offices have real walls.

"You are coming this Sunday. It's your niece's first communion." She wasn't asking a question.

"I'm going away this weekend. I paid a lot of money for a share in a beach house." I flop into the ergonomically calibrated chair and look out of the window. Fifteen stories down, people scurry to and from their jobs, all scrabbling at the pile of cash. My hands are bigger and faster.

"No, mister. You're going to be at your goddaughter's first communion. You're going to spend a few hours with your family. How many months has it been since you've been to church? No one is impressed with your Wall Street job and all the money you make."

Yes they are. "Fine, I'll be there. How's Pop?"

She sighs, and the fight has gone out of her. "Good days and bad days."

My chest tightens and, fuck it all, my eyes burn.

"We should talk about what to do with him."

"There's nothing to do with your father. He is fine at home. We're not going to let strangers care for him in some hospital."

"Momma. It might get to be too much for you. People with Alzheimer's—"

"Shush." She takes a breath so deep I have to hold the phone away from my ear. "We'll see you Sunday."

I end the call and toss my phone on the desk. How much partying do I have to do Saturday at the beach to make Sunday with the Rinaldis bearable?

Chapter 3

GINA

"Gina *mia*, don't forget to take the pill." Nonna hands me the white tablet and a glass of water.

"I don't like it." I stare at the palm of her hand. It has four prominent lines and sixty-three thin ones.

"You told Jennifer you would take the medicine every day." She pushes her hand toward me.

I shake my head. "It made me feel sick the past two days."

Nonna doesn't say anything, and gently takes my hand and places the chalky pill in it. I put it on the back of my tongue. The taste is bitter and I almost gag as I pour the water down my throat.

"Ugh." I wag my head. My back starts to itch like crazy.

"See? Not so bad." Nonna scratches my back, and the itch goes away.

"I don't think it works."

"Have you tried the skills Jennifer taught you?"

"Maybe." I put on my shoes. The laces must be straight, and I retie them three times to make sure.

"Why don't you try the introducing-yourself

skill? All you have to do is say your name." Nonna hands me my lunch bag. There will be two tablespoons of peanut butter and one tablespoon of Nutella. The apple will be cut into eight segments.

"Gina, are you listening?"

"Okay, today I will introduce myself to someone."

"And you can tell everyone at group this afternoon."

I walk to the subway. It is summer, and the sun is up at five fifty-three a.m. But it is still cool. Later the temperature will reach ninety-two degrees, and the humidity will be seventy-six percent.

There is a usual morning rush at the store. Thursdays are busy. Only Fridays slow down over the summer.

"Double-shot caramel mochaccino," Becky calls.

I look at Christopher Rinaldi. He always gets the same thing. I prepare the drink. My back itches, and I wiggle my shoulders trying to ease it.

"Ants in your pants?" Becky asks. But it is the kind of question that you are not supposed to answer. I am surprised I remember that.

Instead of placing the mochaccino on the counter, I hold it out to Christopher. The itch is getting worse, but I made a promise to Nonna.

"Hello, Christopher. I'm Gina Giancarlo." I hold my right hand out, and my left hand extends the drink.

He looks up from his iPhone. "Huh?"

I take a deep breath. "IamGinaGiancarlo. It'snicetomeetyou...Christopher."

His eyes squint, his nose wrinkles, and he looks at my face. Then his face smooths out. "Oh, Regina from Eighty-Second Avenue." He shifts his iPhone, takes my right hand and quickly pumps it, then takes the coffee from me. "I thought I recognized you. Have you been working here long?"

"Three years, five months, and three days."

He laughs and shakes his head. "You always did have a head for numbers."

"Gina, stop flirting. We've got customers."

"See ya, Gina Giancarlo." Christopher walks away.

I relax my face. I was smiling without remembering to smile. That was step three of the skill.

When my shift is over, I say good-bye to Sarah, but not to Becky, because she walks away from me.

The bus that takes me to the Autism Center has an average of twenty-eight people on it, if I calculate the passengers getting on and off at each stop. But there were thirty-one when I got on, and at this stop where I get off, there are thirty-seven. Those are both prime numbers.

"Hello, Gina. You can go back to the testing office first," Amber, the receptionist, says when I enter.

I won't see Jennifer today, because this is a special visit just for the new medicine.

"Gina, have a seat. Do you remember me? Dr. Welsh from Genloran Pharmaceuticals." The tall man who wears plaid button shirts points to a chair across the table from where he got up.

"Yes, Dr. Welsh. I just met you a few weeks ago when we started the study. Why would I forget you?"

"I didn't think you would. You're very bright." He pulls out a stack of cards after we both sit at the green-top table. There are two big scratches in the veneer. "Now, Gina. We're going to do some activities again. Remember, there's no right or wrong answer. We want to measure your reactions."

I wait because he hasn't asked me anything yet.

"Let's start with this one. Can you tell me a story about this picture?"

"That's one of the same pictures you showed me last time. There's a window with six panes of glass, a street outside the window with two cars, and a sun setting behind a hill. Inside, there is a couch and a boy looking out of the window."

"Yes." He pauses and makes some notes on a yellow pad of paper. "Is there any story you can think of?"

My back starts to itch. I know there must be something more he wants me to say, because he is waiting. But I described everything in the picture. He said the word "story." Can there be a story in just one picture?

"The boy is waiting," I say. "He is waiting for someone to come play with him, and no one has come, and now it is almost nighttime and he can't play. He is confused and sad."

Dr. Welsh nods and writes down more notes. He shows me the same pictures as before, but this time I think I say what he wants, because he is scribbling notes fast. The last picture is a woman and child.

"I can't see their faces," I say.

"Yes, you just see their backs. But can you guess about a story?"

"Is it a boy or a girl? Is that a mother or a grandmother?"

"Can you tell from the picture?" Dr. Welsh's pen hovers over his pad.

"I think they are happy because they are walking to the movie theater. They are going to see a funny movie and eat popcorn. The girl is happy to be out with her grandmother." As soon as I say those words, I remember when Nonna took me to see *Lilo and Stitch*. Mother didn't take me because I was older than many of the kids in the theater, but Nonna wanted to see the movie, like I did.

"Gina, you did a nice job today." Dr. Welsh stands and opens the door. "Please go to the nurse's office, and then you can go home."

"Okay. Thank you." I stand and shift on my feet.

"Is it working?"

"I can't really discuss it. And there's no way to know this soon. Do you notice anything different?"

"Maybe." I don't want to tell Dr. Welsh about the skills and my memories. I can tell Jennifer when I see her. Or Nonna.

The nurse's office is down the hall and it is very small. She is kind and apologizes when she takes my blood.

"How have you been feeling since taking the medication?" she asks as she wraps the blood-pressure cuff around my arm.

I anticipate the swelling of the cuff and hold my breath.

"Just relax, Gina." She squeezes the bulb quickly. It's over very soon and I let my breath out.

"I don't feel as nauseous after I take it. I sleep better, too. I don't toss and turn like the first week."

"Great." She smiles and enters what I told her into her laptop.

"How will they know if it works?" I roll my sleeve down and can hear my heart thumping.

"I can't really discuss that. But do you feel different?"

"I don't think I realized what the medication was going to do. I didn't know it would help me to see feelings."

She grins and pulls down another white bottle just like all the ones she's given me previously. "As long as you're feeling healthy and well, that's all that matters right now."

"You don't know which bottle has the placebo, do you? I really want this to work. I didn't care before. But now, I want to be like the people who come into the coffee shop and smile and talk on their phones and meet friends for coffee."

"I think if you want anything bad enough, you can get it." She touches my arm and I stand to leave. "You're a smart young woman, and if you have an ambition, you can reach it."

Can that be true? Can wanting something so much it makes your chest ache be enough to make it come true? And do I have an ambition now?

CHRISTOPHER

Church isn't that bad. It doesn't aggravate my hangover, and because it's first communion, the singing is half decent.

I call up my old trick of appearing to be praying, while really sleeping. A skill I have perfected.

I don't really sleep. Instead, I rewind the tape in my head of the previous night. A smile spreads across my face.

I'm one lucky bastard.

Threesomes usually only happen in porn films, but not last night.

Rob drove me to the train station this morning

and could not stop talking about it.

"How did you manage that?" he repeated over and over.

The reality of a threesome is not as great as it looks. After all, I only have two hands, one mouth, and one cock. It requires a lot more attention than I usually want to put into sex. But I couldn't pass up the opportunity.

I had been flirting with the blonde and the brunette, trying to decide which one to focus in on, when the brunette (I think her name was Jamie) offered herself and her friend.

"Chris, wake up." Rico, the second oldest, nudges me, and I open my eyes. Everyone is filing out of the pew, and I rise to trail after my family.

The walk isn't long from Our Lady of Peace to my parents' house, but because everyone came out for first communion, it takes about twenty minutes to say hello and shake some hands.

The house is packed. I'm the only one not married, and my five older siblings have started breeding. Gravy is bubbling on the stove. At least I'll get a great meal, which will help with the pounding in my head.

"Hey, Christopher, sit here. Tell us about the Hamptons." Rico shifts over on the couch, and he balances baby Joe on his knee.

"What's there to tell?" I slap his back as I sit. With one finger I make an effort to tickle the baby's knee. It's about as much baby contact as I want.

"Come on. Humor me. I got nothing going on since this little guy. I bet you got with some bikini-clad girl." His voice drops so Aunt Sophie can't hear.

I don't say anything, but hold up two fingers.

"Nah, you're lying."

"Didn't little Caroline look precious in her gown?" Aunt Sophie's piping voice cuts through the general murmur.

"Yes, she did." My sister Vicki takes little Joe and holds her against her chest tighter than looks comfortable.

"It was Carina's." My other sister Sherry's voice, barely above a whisper, is heard perfectly because we have all stopped talking.

"You missed the annual softball tournament." Marco comes to the rescue, as always. He's the proud father today, and, as the family peacemaker, ensures the mood stays light.

"Sorry," I say. "I had plans in the Hamptons."

"The Hamptons, the Hamptons." Momma shakes a tomato-sauce-covered spoon at me. "You probably don't even know that Marco got a promotion."

"Way to go, Marc. What are you doing now?"

"Same as before. Only now my delivery route takes me to Manhattan, and I map the routes for the other guys. It gives me extra hours and pay."

"Cool." I nod. Marco's extra hours and pay don't

come close to what I'm bringing in. And everyone knows it. Rarely is there a silence in the house, but we're all thinking the same thing. I went to college and made a big shot of myself, and everyone else is stuck in Kew Gardens.

"Where's Pop?" I look around.

"It's easier for him to sit out back. When there's a big crowd in the house, it agitates him."

I nod.

"Go see him."

I nod again and squeeze past the women who are spilling out of the kitchen shuttling dishes to the table.

My father sits in a chair on the screened-in back porch, alone. The sunlight is coming through and reflects off the white wisps of hair that fly away from his head.

I pull up a wicker chair next to him.

"Hi, Pop."

He turns his head from where he has been staring into the backyard. His eyes travel around my face without meeting mine. He looks down at my shorts and shoes, searching for a clue.

"It's me, Christofo." Crap, I hate that my voice cracks and my throat burns.

"I know who you are!" He pounds his fist on the arm of the chair. "They're all here, aren't they? Making noise, making a mess."

"All the kids are here, Pop. Your grandkids,

too." I turn to look at the backyard. How many games of catch were played back there? How many thumpings did I get from my older brothers? Always the youngest boy, always the smallest. Now I had something to show them. "I went to the Hamptons this weekend, Pop. I make good money at my job."

"Bah!"

"Do you want something to eat?"

"Of course I do. Are they trying to starve me?"

Grateful for an excuse, I get up and return to the kitchen. I convince my sister Vikki to give Pop his plate of food.

After everything is brought to the table, we sit.

"Rico, say Grace," Momma commands.

While Rico's words pour out in an automatic cadence, I realize I've got a lot to be thankful for. I don't live in Queens, I'm not tied to one woman whose hips are spreading from pushing out pups, and I make more money than all my brothers put together. The food is a welcome thing as well.

A meal at the Rinaldis' is never a quiet affair. The passing of dishes, the loud exchanges. I sit back and take it in. There's always a spot for me at this table, but no longer a place.

"Chris, tell us about life on Wall Street," Donny, the oldest, says.

I swallow the huge mouthful of pasta with gravy and scramble for something I could share that wouldn't demean me in the eyes of my mother, or make it seem like I am as far removed from my old life as I actually am.

"I ran into Regina Giancarlo at a coffee shop near work."

This creates a crash of silence. Momma's right hand flies to make the sign of the cross, and her lips move in soundless prayer.

I look to the left and right, but all my family avoids my gaze.

"What? Does she still live up the block?"

"You never knew what happened?" Vikki's voice is strained, and a tear spills over her face.

"That retarded girl!" Rico spits.

"She's not retarded. She's actually really smart—" Donny says.

"Shush!" Momma orders. "Gina moved out when her mother abandoned her. She lives with her grandmother in Rego Park. Has for the past six years."

Six is the sacred number. Next year it will be seven. That's how we count in our family—the number of years since Carina died because of my negligence.

Chapter 4

GINA

All the seats in the group room are taken. All six members came to group today. Even Allan, who almost never comes.

"It makes me throw up," Kyle complains.

"Yes, one of the side effects of the medication is nausea. And it's tough because you have to take it on an empty stomach." Jennifer writes down that Kyle complained about vomiting.

She needs to keep track of everything we say about the new medicine, so the scientists can study what happens when we take it.

"I practiced more skills this week," I volunteer. "I introduced myself to a new person. When I introduced myself to Christopher last week, it didn't count because I already knew him."

Jennifer laughs. "It counts because you tried, and you followed the steps. How did the skills go this week?"

I laugh back by pushing air through my throat. But it's little bursts, and they feel easier than when I did it before. "I shook our new neighbor's hand and said my name. Her name is Samantha, and she is getting married. Her boyfriend is moving in, too."

"Wow, sounds like you had a whole conversation," Jennifer says.

"It lasted seven minutes and twenty seconds."

"I practiced skills. I practiced skills." Jerome rocks in his seat. He says everything twice. It would only count as one skill even if he said it twice. I feel my mouth form a smile at the funny thought.

"What skill did you practice?" Jennifer asks.

Jerome stops rocking and pulls at his hair.

"Jerome doesn't always understand what we're talking about, does he?" I ask. When I think back, even though Jerome says things twice, he's never really followed along with the conversation. "That's not fair." I rub my back against the chair to scratch it. "The rest of us have to stay on the topic, but Jerome never does."

Jennifer turns to face me. Her eyes are wide open.

"You're surprised about something," I say.

I rub my back harder.

"It's okay, Gina. You did a beautiful job of letting us know why you are angry." She laughs a small laugh. "Some people go their whole lives without expressing their anger appropriately."

"And I noticed you were surprised." I stop rubbing my back.

"You did." She makes a note on her clipboard.

The rest of the group seems to take longer than usual. Everyone gets a turn talking about the social skills they practiced. But no one really did them like I did. It seems like we were all Level Ones, but somehow I'm a Level One-half. It feels like a big balloon is blowing up inside my chest, but in a comfortable way that makes me sit up and stop itching.

Finally, it ends. The clock says four-thirty, which is the time group always ends, but that felt like a lot longer.

I get up to leave, and Jennifer tells me to wait a minute.

"Gina, do you feel different since taking the new medicine?"

I shrug.

"Because I notice a big change. Not only are you practicing your social skills, you're also expressing emotions."

"Okay."

"I found something for you." She reaches into her bag and pulls out a thick book. "I found it at a yard sale and thought of you. It's a textbook for a design class."

It is heavy. The cover is thick cardboard, and the pages are crinkly. "It's like books from school."

"Exactly. Only this one was from a school where they taught people about interior design."

"Why would someone need to learn that?"

"Not everyone has your gift of arranging a room."

"This room is still set up wrong." I look around at the chairs and imagine how it would be if we were allowed to move them. To place them so there was more space. We could add tables and floor lamps. And break up the room so there were small areas for sitting.

"I know. But take a look at this and maybe it will give you more ideas."

"Thank you very much. I appreciate the gift." I smile, because I remembered the "Saying Thank You" skill, and because when Jennifer gave me the book, the balloon in my chest got a little bit bigger.

CHRISTOPHER

I avoided the coffee shop for a week. I tried the place near work, but ran into too many people from the office. I had to order large coffees and couldn't add any sugar with Stan and Will hovering at my shoulder trying to glean my latest bit of gossip from the coal industry.

But screw it — whatever the reason my family hated Regina Giancarlo, it has nothing to do with me. The Rinaldis carry grudges for slights dating back to Sicily. Whatever coincidence there is between Gina and Carina wouldn't mean my vision would be clouded with the image of my sister's limp body every time I looked at Gina.

I walk in and place my usual order. I step to the side and watch Gina as she works.

She doesn't waste a movement, every action precise and calculated. She looks a little different than last I saw her. Certainly different than I remember her.

She isn't retarded, as Rico said. She has autism, and she was in my grade but didn't go to Our Lady of Peace with the rest of the kids from the block. She went to the public school where she apparently kicked ass in math class, according to Scott, the Jewish kid from around the corner who also went to the public school.

I always remember her walking with her gaze straight ahead. She didn't seem to notice things, like people nodding hello or calling to each other. But I did remember once when Old Lady Cotraccia couldn't find her car, Gina could tell her how many cars down the block it was and recite the license plate. Old Lady Cotraccia didn't even know her license number.

Now, Gina hums along with the eighties rock song and bobs her head in time to the music as she works the milk steamer. Her hair is a crazy shade of reddish brown that on another woman I'd want verification. Her makeup is a little heavy, but nothing I didn't see in Queens.

"Here you are, Christopher Rinaldi." She hands

me the cup instead of setting it on the counter.

"You can just call me Chris." I take the cup and notice that her fingers are stained brown from hair dye. Guess I don't need verification.

"Furniture stain red mahogany." She keeps intense eye contact that makes me step back.

"Huh?"

"I was refinishing a table Nonna and I bought at a yard sale. To match a side table we already have." She wiggles her fingers and examines them. "I like redecorating the house."

"Sounds like fun."

She looks at me again with a severity I expect from an irate day trader who lost his shirt on my intel. Then she smiles, and her face relaxes. She picks up another cup, reads the order, and goes back to work.

"It's one of my hobbies. I also keep track of our stock portfolio." She steams a pitcher of milk as she talks.

"No kidding?"

"No, I'm not kidding." She stops stirring and looks up. Her green eyes flash into my gut. With a little less makeup, she'd be stunning. "Nonna has my grandfather's pension, and with her social security we have invested a third in mutual funds, a third in long-term bonds, and a third in gold."

"That way you minimize your risk. I work for Humbolt and Sutter."

"Are you a trader or an analyst?" She places cup after cup effortlessly on the counter. Filling each order with mechanized precision. The wave of customers doesn't fluster her a bit. Her cool demeanor doesn't falter.

"Analyst. You would be good at it with your head for numbers."

"I like designing." She jerks her head up, almost as if she has surprised herself. "Yes, that's what I really like doing."

"Then you should do it."

"Decaf cappuccino. Come on, Gina. Pick it up." A shrill woman with "Becky" pinned to her apron barks at Gina, who has slowed for only a moment to ponder a career vastly more interesting than pouring espressos.

"I should get out of your way. Good-bye, Gina."

She freezes and looks up in panic. "I forgot to tell you good-bye." She takes a deep breath. "Good-bye, Chris. It was nice seeing you again," she recites, as if learning to speak English.

I chuckle. "Yeah, Gina. It was nice to see you, too."

Chapter 5

GINA

Even though I know what pictures Dr. Welsh is going to show me, I'm shocked when I set my eyes on the boy standing by the window. Emotions bloom from every line.

"Can you tell me a story about this picture?" he asks, with his pen ready.

"It's the morning and the sun is rising. The boy can't wait to go to his first day of school. Any minute his friends will come by and he will rush outside to join them. When he does, they'll all greet him with high fives, and then they skip down the block. His mother has packed his favorite lunch, but he'll swap the chips for an apple with his best friend because his best friend never gets chips."

Dr. Welsh hasn't written a word. "What made you think of that story? Was it a movie or a book?"

"No. I don't think it's something I saw. It's just something I thought up. Last time I thought it was a sunset and a sad picture. But there's no reason it can't be a happy picture. Is there? Am I allowed to change my mind about it?" I grow a little warm. If I mess this up, will they take the pills away?

"No, of course you're allowed to change your mind. In fact, you should approach the pictures with a fresh start each time." He writes his notes with his head bent over the paper.

"It's working, isn't it? I can't possibly be taking the placebo. How many other people are making progress?" I sit up straighter and think of all the times throughout the day when I noticed little things I never was aware of before. People's facial expressions, the changes in the tone of their voices.

"Let's finish the test, shall we?"

I put my all into each picture, trying to make each one more complex than the last.

Dr. Welsh says good-bye and directs me to the nurse.

She goes through the routine of taking a blood sample, measuring my blood pressure, and asking about side effects.

"I think you're right," I tell her as I stand in the doorway, ready to leave.

"About what, Gina?"

"I think if you want something enough, and really work at it, you can make anything happen."

She smiles. "You're a smart woman, and brave for doing this. A little faith can go a long way."

Jennifer's office door is open, and she is sitting at her desk.

"Jennifer, do you have time to talk?"

"I've got a few minutes. I'd love to hear how you're doing."

"Do you think the medicine is working? You're my social worker, I'm pretty sure you have to tell me the truth."

"Gina, I love your honesty. I have no idea what has caused the change in you. But you have changed. You know it, don't you?"

I tell her about the skills I've used, about Chris, about the pictures and some of the memories they bring up. "That's not how I used to think."

"No, it's not. Certainly, it could be the drug. But you're also working harder than ever. Are you happy about the change?"

"I want so much to have these things other people have. Friends, real friends. People have conversations in the coffee shop about their husbands and children. They talk about vacations they take, or their jobs."

"One step at a time, Gina. I'm really proud of you. No matter what the drug does or doesn't do, you are the one who has to make these things happen."

When I get up to leave, she stands too. I hug her, because people who care about each other hug. I see women in the coffee shop hug each other hello and good-bye. So I grab Jennifer around her arms and squeeze.

"Oof." Jennifer steps back.

"I didn't do that right."

"Well, I wasn't expecting it, and generally, you don't hug so tightly. But thank you for the affection."

"Thank you for letting me hug you."

The subway ride home is a chance for me to study people. Why do some couples hold hands and talk quietly together, while some sit side by side and don't even look at each other? Why do some parents read small books to their children and some text on the phone and don't watch as their kids pick at dried gum on the seat? I don't think I ever noticed the differences in how people act.

Is there a right and wrong way to have a friendship? I walk from the subway to our house. I don't even count the steps as I climb the stoop.

Nonna is sitting in her easy chair.

"I told Jennifer all about the skills I used today. She was very proud." I come into the living room. The new table looks great. It complements the cream-colored slipcover I sewed this weekend.

"Gina, I'm so proud, too." Nonna's face changes. Her smile is so light, and her eyes crinkle.

I giggle, because she looks younger than she is. Giggling is a new kind of laughing I do. It jiggles the balloon in my chest and makes me feel younger. I flop on the couch next to her.

"Tell me about your social skills." She pats my hand.

"I had an entire conversation with a customer. I told him about refinishing the table and made eye contact the entire time." I look at the corner of the room and notice we need a new accent piece. "I forgot to say good-bye. But Chris reminded me, and then I did, and said it was nice to see him again."

"Chris?"

"Christopher Rinaldi. He likes to be called Chris. He used to live —"

"I remember him, Regina." Nonna stares into the distance. It's hard to know what a person is thinking when they don't say or do anything. But I realize that she is thinking. She's working on what she wants to say back to me.

The itching on my back starts. Something is wrong. Before the pills, I would have never noticed something was wrong if Nonna was silent.

"It's good you're getting better at your social skills, but I don't want you to get too friendly with Christopher."

"Why not?"

"He's from your past. You've got a bright new future ahead of you."

The balloon in my chest pulses. Heat rises inside my head; there is pounding.

"But Chris is friendly to me. He talks to me. The other customers don't."

"If you have to, you can find another job. But you can't be friends with him."

"No." My voice scares me, and I leap from the couch.

"Come here, Gina *mia*. I'll scratch your back."

"My back doesn't itch." And it doesn't. I'm angry. I'm upset, but my back doesn't itch. I don't understand.

Nonna shakes her head. "Those pills woke something inside you. It's difficult to learn what to do with your feelings."

"The only difficult thing is that you won't let me be friends with Chris Rinaldi if I want." I stomp up the stairs to my room and slam the door. It rattles in the frame, and my mouth drops open. When was the last time I yelled at Nonna? I can't remember any time ever. Did I ever yell at anyone?

I sit on the edge of my bed and survey the room. Recently, I chose a nautical theme that I saw in an issue of *Better Homes*. The furnishings and placement were as exact as I could get to the picture taped to the edge of my vanity mirror.

Why can't I make my own designs? The book Jennifer gave me doesn't lay out step by step how to design and decorate a room. It gives general ideas. I could have my own ideas.

And one of my ideas is to be friends with Chris.

CHRIS

"And tell me why you're recommending Genloran

Pharmaceuticals at this time?" Bob Breckner, vice president of market analysis, eyes me over his computer screen.

I perch in one of the leather chairs that should be comfortable and luxurious. Instead, I expect the stiff upholstery to propel me out of the seat.

"They're in phase three trials of a new psychiatric drug. It looks very promising as a treatment for some kinds of cognitive disorders. Some are saying maybe even a cure."

Bob's eyebrows lift even higher. "Psychiatric drugs aren't big moneymakers. Cancer, diabetes, even heart disease. But crazy pills? Maybe for depression. Good God, everyone is depressed, but cognitive disorders?"

I have to salvage this. I need a breakout move.

"Someone in my expert network —"

He holds up his hand. "Let me stop you there. I know how expert networks operate, and I'm sure our company has made a fortune off them. But it skirts the edge of insider trading. The SEC has come down hard recently on experts. So before you go any further, think about what you are going to tell me. Are you about to tell me something that could land either of us in an FBI interrogation room? Or is your 'expert'" —he puts air quotes around that word—"a true expert with no ties to Genloran?"

I swallow hard because my mouth has gone dry. This could be the move that makes me stand out from the pack.

When my old frat buddy called and invited me out for a drink, I had no idea he had been laid off from a competing pharmaceutical company. He told me about how he had lost the development race to Genloran's R&D department. He was looking for a little cash to tide him over until he could find more work. It seemed like money well spent.

"My expert was never employed at Genloran. He had a job—"

Bob holds up his hand again. "Let me tell you how this works, Chris. If you want to base recommendations on an old high school buddy, that's fine, but—"

"We were frat brothers."

"Stop talking." Bob shakes his head. "What I'm trying to tell you is that I don't want to know who he is or what he said. Do you understand?"

"Sure." My mood lightens, because it looks like Bob's going to give me the green light.

"No, you don't understand. It's on your shoulders. You are recommending our traders buy huge amounts of this stock based on information only you know about. I don't know about it, none of the other analysts know about it…"

I might not be the brightest bulb, but even I figure out that Bob is telling me I'm going to be hung out to dry if this goes south.

Do or die. I'm never going to get the big payoff if

I don't take the big risks.

"Sure, Bob. I understand. I think this would be too big an opportunity to pass up. Little Genloran is going to hit this out of the park and probably get bought by one of the big pharma companies. Anyone with Genloran stock is going to get very rich."

Bob smiles as if he's just sipped an expensive brandy. "That's what I like to hear. We're all about getting rich."

I stand, thankful for the chance to leave.

"By the way, you're coming to the July Fourth party?"

"Wouldn't miss it." The company rents out a cruise ship for the analysts and traders to watch the fireworks from out in New York Harbor.

"Excellent. Bring a date." Bob turns his attention to one of his computer screens.

"Uh. I'm not seeing anyone right now."

"Doesn't matter." He doesn't look up. "The partners like to see you bring a date to make sure you're not going to get drunk and make out with one of the interns. Or the hot chicks from legal. Why are all the young female lawyers so sexy?" He shakes his head. "Bring someone to impress the partners."

"Um, okay." I figure I'm dismissed, so I shut his door, which closes soundlessly.

Great—where am I going to find a date in two days? I didn't save any numbers of any of the women I've been with lately. Who knew I'd need one of them again?

I could ask Rob, but he'd bring one of his intellectually ambiguous girls he meets at bus stops.

I need someone who can understand economics, someone who won't go all crazy and lose control.

Someone like Gina Giancarlo.

Chapter 6

GINA

Chris comes in while I rinse out the stainless steel milk carafes. He never comes in during the middle of the day.

I smile, and that balloon swells in my chest.

For about two weeks, he has had a short conversation with me when I hand him his drink. *About two weeks?* I quickly calculate that it's been eight days, not including the weekends.

We talk about the business page in the paper. I recite the closing numbers of certain stocks we're both tracking. He encourages me to take more risk with Nonna's money, and I warn him about being over-leveraged. It's become a comfortable kind of conversation. I don't even have to think about the skills anymore; they just happen with Chris.

Nonna's words come back to me, but for some reason it only makes me want to befriend him even more.

I believed I had friends before, but now I know friendship means more than walking side by side wordlessly or going up and down on the seesaw until the other person says they have to go.

"Hello, Chris." I feel warm when he walks up to me.

"Hey, Gina. I hoped that you'd still be here."

"On Fridays, I work until four p.m." I dry the carafe and keep myself from moving to put it away. When you're involved in a conversation, it's important to stay facing the person and make eye contact.

"Listen, I need a favor. We're friends, right?"

That balloon is about to burst apart. "Yes, we're friends." My voice is barely above a whisper.

"Are you doing anything on the Fourth of July?"

"On the Fourth of July, Nonna and I watch the parade on Seventy-Sixth Avenue, then we watch the fireworks on TV."

"How would you like to see the fireworks in person from a boat?" His smile beams.

"I don't know. It never occurred to me to do something different."

"The company I work for has a big party on a boat. There's food and music and as much booze as you want."

"I-I can't drink alcohol." Jennifer says it's very important not to drink alcohol while taking the new pills. I don't tell Chris about the pills. I don't think it's something I'm supposed to share with friends.

"Oh, uh, that's okay. You can have whatever you want to drink. We each need to bring a friend, and I thought you might like to go." He puts his hands in his pockets and takes a step back.

"Can Nonna come?"

"Sorry." He shifts his feet and looks around the shop.

A few customers come in, and Sarah takes their orders. She signals to me that she will get the drinks.

This is what friendship is. Doing social activities. I haven't been to a real party in years. The birthday parties Nonna gives me don't count, because the only people who come are my aunt and uncle and cousins. No friends.

"Yes. I want to go to the party on the boat."

"Great. Oh, do you have a dress?"

I nod.

"Not an ordinary dress. It has to be —"

"I'll help her get one," Sarah chimes in. "We'll go shopping."

Chris lets out a long breath. "Thanks." He takes out his iPhone. "Give me your address, and I'll have a car come and get you."

"A car?"

"Yeah, to bring you back and forth to the party."

I recite my address, and he shakes my hand.

"You're doing me a huge favor," he says.

"What are friends for?" I heard that on a few television shows.

He laughs and leaves.

"Va va va voom." Sarah slaps me on the back.

"What?"

"You've got a date with that hot guy who has been flirting with you for the past few weeks."

"Eight days," I correct her.

"Oh, no, no, no. You are not going back to that." Sarah pulls me to the end of the counter so the customers can't hear. "I don't know what's come over you, but you're a different person these days."

I wiggle my back, because I think I should tell her about the medicine, but maybe not.

"And don't start with your back again. You're smiling naturally to customers, you talk with a natural voice, and you've got a date with a cute guy."

"He's my friend. He said I'm doing him a favor."

She rolls her eyes, which means she doesn't believe me. "It might start as doing a favor for him, but it can grow into something more." She waggles her eyebrows.

I laugh, and I don't even have to think about how to do it.

"Come on. As soon as the afternoon shift arrives, we're going shopping to get you a dress."

"Why are you doing that for me?"

"Because that's what friends are for."

CHRIS

I pace back and forth in front of the gangplank. This is a bad idea. I should have come alone. I should have gotten one of Rob's girls. He showed up five minutes ago with an unnatural redhead on platform heels and a ribbon dress that she kept tugging down to cover her butt and yanking up to cover her tits.

But Rob doesn't care about advancement. He doesn't care if he makes a good impression. His date could be dimmer than the dinner rolls, and he'd still be a trader and still have the life he wants.

I have my eye on VP. Bob Breckner can't live forever.

Gina seemed like a good choice, given my options. She's not nearly as awkward as I remember her. She has interests outside of the coffee shop. Always talking about interior design. And she catches on quick to any subject. Whenever we talk about my job, she grasps ideas that took me semesters at Wharton to understand.

But maybe she's too strange for this group. Hopefully, everyone will get shit-faced soon and not notice.

A sedan pulls up and the rear door opens. A woman in a black cocktail dress gets out. Her shapely legs start with a pair of black baby-doll shoes and end below the mid-thigh hem of a dress that clings to full hips, but not so tightly that my imagination can't go to work.

A choker of silver beads surround an elegant neck, and teardrop earrings hang from ears half hidden from piles of chestnut curls.

"Hello, Chris."

"Gina?"

"Am I okay? Sarah said this dress was the right kind." She stands in place with a death grip on her purse.

I walk toward her and take her arm. "You look fabulous. I didn't recognize you. Wait, that didn't come out right."

"Why?" She allows me to guide her toward the ramp up to the boat.

"It sounded like I said you don't always look fabulous. Not that I want you to think I'm thinking about how you look. I-I..."

Gina's face screws up in confusion. "But I don't always look like this. I usually wear an apron over my jeans at work."

I laugh. "I know. Come on, I'll introduce you around."

In some ways, Gina could be the perfect date. We're friends, so she couldn't care less if I think she is attractive, and she doesn't get the subtleties of language if I slip up like I just did.

Everyone has a drink in hand. The band plays grotesque rock versions of patriotic songs. And Gina negotiates the steps without much tottering on her heels.

"Chris, come here." Bob Breckner waves me toward the group he stands among. Not only the VP from sales but the CFO as well.

We make introductions, including each of their heavily Botoxed wives. They each drip with gold and jewels, and although their bodies are perfectly toned and sculpted through Pilates and a surgeon's knife, none of them are sexy.

"Gina, your dress is…classic." Bob's wife eyes her up and down. "You don't see them like that anymore."

"I saw plenty of them on the rack at JCPenney yesterday." Gina's tone is as matter-of-fact as you could get. I nearly choke trying to hide my laughter, but of course she doesn't mean it as anything more than fact.

"Gina, what do you do?" Bob asks.

"I work at Perks Plus."

"But she's studying interior design," I inject. I didn't think that part through, but it wasn't a lie, and I hope the pressure I put on her back is enough signal to send Gina the message to go along.

"That's true," she says. "I'm reading a textbook right now called *Fundamentals of Interior Design*. My nonna lets me rearrange the furniture in the house whenever I want." Gina takes the glass of wine I hand her but then holds it at arm's length, threatening to spill it on the sequined dress of the CFO's wife.

I take the wine back. Asking her to pretend to drink is a bit too much.

"Your nonna?" the CFO asks.

"Gina lives with her grandmother. Helps care for her, you know, so the woman doesn't have to go into a home," I explain, with more pressure on Gina's back.

"But we do live in a home." Luckily, Gina's words are drowned out by the ship's horn. We're pulling away from the dock and headed to the southern tip of Manhattan.

We all move to the railing to watch our departure.

Gina smiles and claps, and I feel my cheeks pull into a grin as well. We might be able to fake it tonight.

When the excitement dies down, conversation turns to work. The women study their drinks and the skyline, but Gina is intent on the discussion.

"And that's a twenty-three percent decrease in return from last year. Which isn't bad, considering the hit other firms took," Bob says.

"Thirty-four percent," Gina says.

All heads turn to her.

"What?" Bob asks.

"If the numbers you stated were accurate, it's a thirty-four percent decrease." She takes a sip of the ginger ale I got for her.

"Gina has a head for numbers," I explain.

Bob has taken his phone out of his pocket and made some calculations. "What do you know, she's right." He grins sheepishly. "I guess we took more of a hit than I thought."

The CFO scowls, but the moment is saved when a waiter appears with a tray of bacon-wrapped figs.

Gina takes four off the tray before I can stop her.

And I catch some raised eyebrows as I excuse us.

"You're only supposed to take one at a time," I hiss.

"Why? I'm hungry," she says around a fig.

"Chris, my man." Rob appears with his date in tow. She has perfected the too-bored-to-be-impressed look.

"Hey, Rob. This is Gina."

Rob eyes her up and down and gives me a thumbs-up.

Gina studies her own legs and cleavage. "What are you looking at?" she asks him.

Rob chuckles and turns beet red. His date cocks her head to the side, but has decided that Gina is no competition and trains her attention on her flute of champagne.

"Do you like my dress?" Gina looks herself over again.

"Yes. I mean, no." Rob turns to me for help. But I'm enjoying his discomfort.

Commotion on the opposite side of the ship interrupts our conversation.

The fireworks are about to start, and I can only hope this evening doesn't bring any more embarrassing moments.

Chapter 7

GINA

Fireworks shake your insides when you're close to them. The booms echo against the high-rises. I can feel the music pounding in my legs. This is way better than watching with Nonna.

Thinking of her gives me a pang, an uncomfortable tug on the balloon. She's at Aunt Sophia's tonight, and they are eating hot dogs and watching the fireworks on TV. She is not happy that I am out with Chris. And saying good-bye to her was weird. She almost forbade me from going. But even if she didn't give me permission, I was going to go anyway.

Sarah and I spent hours trying on dresses, and Chris paid for a car to pick me up. And for the first time there was something I really, truly yearned for. Not something I wanted, like a new area rug, but something that pulled at my insides. Something where I wasn't going to feel complete unless I had it.

And here I am. All the women wear fancy dresses, and even though mine doesn't have sparkles, it's a good one. A classic, is what that woman called it. I smile as a bunch of fizzling fireworks dissipate in the sky.

"Cool, huh?" Chris stands just behind me, looking over my shoulder. There is a crowd, so he's pressed against my back. But I don't itch. It kinda feels nice, especially in a crush of people, to have a friend next to me.

The fireworks end, and the boat turns around to go back. There are more conversations with people Chris works with. I do my best to remember all the skills, but there are some things you can't practice for.

Like when his boss asks me to do some computations in front of everyone. I don't think he's being friendly. It seems more like when Becky tells me to get a large number of cups from the closet. It's not difficult for me, but I don't think Becky or Chris's boss are respectful of my skills.

The boat bumps against the pier when we get back, and I can hardly balance in the shoes Sarah picked out. She insisted that I needed to wear shoes with a high heel. I wobble and fall into Chris's arms.

"Thanks," I say as he helps me straighten up. I look at him, and his face has gone serious. Maybe I made another mistake by falling, but I couldn't help it.

His Adam's apple jumps in his throat. "You okay?"

I nod, and follow him off the boat.

The same car is there waiting for me.

"I'll ride home with you to make sure you get back safely." He climbs in next to me, gives the driver my address, and leans his head back against the seat.

"I've been in plenty of taxis before, but this is way nicer." I rub my hand over the velvety seat.

"Uh-huh." He keeps his eyes closed.

"I made some mistakes." Once when I was little, I knocked over a bowl that had fake flowers in it. My mother shrieked, which hurt my ears, and I ran to my room. But even that time doesn't compare to what it feels like now. I try to take a deep breath, but it comes in all jumpy and I notice tears on my cheeks.

"Hey, hey. Quit that." Chris uses his thumb to wipe away the tears. "I'm not upset with you. It was a tough gig tonight. Sorry I put you through it. I just thought it would be easier to bring a friend rather than a girl."

"But I am a girl." No matter how many pills I take, I will never understand why people say things that contradict themselves.

Chris laughs. "That's why I like you, Gina. You're a straight shooter. You say what you mean and nothing anyone says bothers you."

"Your boss bothers me."

"Yeah, he bothers me, too." He turns to look out the window, and the lights go flashing past. People are spilling out into the streets from the bars singing

"Yankee Doodle." "But I'm not angry with you. I hate those events. It's all about kissing ass, and I'm not good at that."

"Kissing ass means being nice to people you don't want to be nice to. Like your boss."

"That's right."

"Nonna has always said to be nice to everyone. Even people who are mean and people who make fun of me. I know they do, but I'm nice back because I would never want to be mean."

Chris turns to face me. "You're smarter than most people I know." He places his hand on mine and lays his head back again.

I stare at our hands. Friends hold hands, I know that. But with Chris's hand on mine, I feel friendship doubled.

We don't talk, and I wish we had taken the bridge instead of the Midtown Tunnel so I could enjoy every second of being in a nice car.

"I forget how it's like a small town." Chris has woken up and is looking out the window again. "We could be in another universe instead of across the river."

"I like Queens. I know where everything is. And it's easy to get to work and the Autism Center."

"Yeah." Chris turns to me. He has that serious look again. I couldn't have done anything wrong by sitting here. His eyes drop to my dress, and he shakes his head as if there are mosquitoes buzzing around. "I must have had too much to drink."

"You need to pee?"

He laughs with his head bent down. When he brings his face up, it is very close to mine. I can smell the wine he drank, and that he uses cologne with sandalwood, because we have soap like that.

His lips come very close to my mouth. I try to keep my eyes on them but they cross, and I have to close them. Before I know it, his mouth presses against mine and his lips part, and mine do, too. He puts his tongue inside, and I forget to think. I breathe hard and the blood in my veins pulses. His tongue sweeps around my mouth, and I taste him the same way. He pulls back.

"Shit, sorry." He runs his hand through his hair.

"It's okay. I liked it."

"But friends aren't supposed to—"

"You would kiss someone who wasn't your friend?"

He nods. "You're right. But we're friends, okay?"

"I know that, Chris Rinaldi. You're my best friend." I lay my head back against the plush seat. It is a nice way to relax and think about things.

The car stops in front of my house. Nonna has left the porch light on. Chris gets out and holds the door for me. I fish my key from my purse.

"Good night, Gina. Thanks so much for coming with me."

"I had a lot of fun. And thanks for the kiss. That was fun, too." I walk up the steps with a bit of difficulty, because the stupid shoes Sarah made me buy are starting to hurt.

He waves and watches as I unlock the door.

The television is on and Nonna has fallen asleep on the couch in front of it. I switch it off and cover her with the afghan that brings out the red in the carpet.

Up in my room, I undress and think that between Sarah and Chris, I have some excellent friends. And with this new medicine, I'm learning how to be a friend back.

CHRIS

I approach the coffee shop. My gut twists.

If I were smart, I'd go to the coffee shop two blocks closer to work and suffer with a regular coffee. Then I wouldn't have to face Gina a mere three days after the party.

Stupid.

It was one kiss and didn't mean anything.

But has Gina taken it to mean more than it was? She probably hasn't had many kisses in her life. And it isn't fair to lead her on.

And why did I turn it over in my mind a million times the past two nights? It wasn't as if it was anything special. It was a kiss. Hell, I've kissed plenty of girls and never given any of them a second thought.

Maybe she won't put too much importance on it. After all, she seems to not put too much importance on anything.

I step inside and wait in line. Gina's impressive pace behind the counter keeps the line moving rapidly. Her auburn hair is pulled back into a ponytail that bounces along as she moves in time to the music. Maybe I let the martinis get to me that night, but she's hotter than I remember her being when we were kids.

Before I know it, I place my usual order.

Gina lifts her head when she hears my voice.

"Hi, Chris."

"Hey, Gina. How are you?"

"I'm good. How are you today?" Her large green eyes are framed with thick lashes.

I laugh. "You always sound so proper."

Her face screws up in confusion. For a moment I think smoke will pour out of her ears. Then her features relax, and a smile spreads across her full lips. "You mean I don't sound like a friend." She nods. "I'll work on that."

I can't help but smile back. Her honesty and forthright speech are so welcome from a woman.

"I can't hang around this morning." I glance at my phone. Today is not a day to be late. I want to see how many shares of Genloran we bought.

"Then you should go to work." Gina's tone is calm and natural. Another woman would put an edge of sarcasm in there to try to send a message about how she doesn't want me to leave. I'd have to try to decode the message, and I would fail miserably.

"Okay. How about I drop by your house this Sunday, on my way back from the beach?"

"I would enjoy a visit from you, Chris." When she smiles, she beams a truly joyful energy.

"I'll enjoy it, too." I raise my hand and leave.

The side-eye from the other barista gives me pause, and heat floods my cheeks. I don't get embarrassed. Not ever. Except now.

Outside, I almost smack myself in the head. What the heck was I thinking? There is no reason I should pursue a friendship with Gina, and certainly no reason to seek anything *more* than a friendship. But her sincerity and easy manner just keep drawing me in.

Chapter 8

GINA

The morning rush dies down, and I finally have time to clean some of the milk that always drips down the side of the counter.

"I'm impressed, Gina. You've got Chris practically eating out of your hand." Sarah wipes the counter near me.

"That's an expression that means I have some control over him. But I don't. I didn't tell him to come to the shop."

"What about your date for Sunday?" Sarah waggles her eyebrows.

"Date?"

"He's going to stop by your house for a *visit*." Her emphasis on the last word sends my brain running through all of Jennifer's tips on decoding speech.

"Sarah." I sigh. "Please help me."

She nods and pulls me aside, leaving Becky to handle the stray customers. "When a guy looks at you the way Chris looked at you, when a guy wants to come to your house, it means *something*."

"But what does something mean?" I slap my hands on the table.

"Well, I don't know exactly..." The grin leaves her face, and she chews her lip.

"Chris and I are friends. He said so after we kissed. I'm sure he wants to be friends, because he keeps talking to me and starting conversations, and now he asked to come over."

"Whoa, whoa. You kissed him?"

"Yes, in the car on the way home from the Fourth of July party."

"What kind of kiss?"

"A movie kiss, where we put our tongues in each other's mouths."

Sarah gasps. "And he said he wanted to be friends after the kiss?"

"Of course. He's not going to kiss someone he doesn't want to be friends with." Sometimes Sarah can be as clueless as I am.

She takes a deep breath. "Men are so hard to understand sometimes. And they say we're not the straightforward ones. Listen, that kind of kiss is only for boyfriends and girlfriends. You know that, right?"

I shrug. "Yeah, I do know that. But Chris and I aren't boyfriend and girlfriend. And you're my friend, but I wouldn't kiss you that way." I rest my face in my hands.

"Relationships are tough."

"Tell me about it," I mumble into my palms. And then I bolt up. "Sarah, I used a colloquialism. 'Tell me about it.' That's not formal at all." I feel my face split apart into a smile. I almost tell Sarah about the medicine, and how it's got to be the most amazing thing ever.

"I don't know what you're learning in that Autism Center, but it's working." Sarah stands and puts her hand on my shoulder. "Chris seems like a nice guy. But all guys are interested in being more than friends, no matter what they say."

"He wants to have sex?"

"Shhh." Sarah looks around. "Yes, but also he may not want to. I don't want you to get hurt, but I also want you to enjoy the attention he's giving you."

I shake my head. "I don't think they cover this situation at the Autism Center."

GINA

I walk into our group room, and it doesn't even bother me today that the chairs and tables are helter-skelter. I'm beginning to understand that not everyone can see space the way I do.

Jennifer walks in first. "Oh, Gina. I'm glad you're here early."

"You must have something you want to talk to me about before everyone else gets here." I sit up straighter.

"You're right. And you know what, that's what I want to talk to you about. Genloran has heard about your progress, and they want to meet you to interview you for an article."

"Like in a newspaper?"

"Similar. But in a medical journal."

I shrug. "Okay. I feel confident about my social skills now. Especially because I have two friends." I pause and picture Sarah's furrowed brow. "Jennifer, do you understand men?"

She sighs. "Not as much as I'd like to. But give me a shot."

"You can't trick me with that saying. I know it means give you a chance to answer my question." I try to think about what my question is. "Chris says he's my friend. And he talks to me like a friend. We went to a party together, and he was friendly. And he kissed me. A boyfriend kiss, with tongue. It was wet."

Jennifer's smile becomes set on her face. It's not her usual smile. "Gina, I know you want to be friends with Chris. But he may not be the best person to be friends with."

I feel heat in my head. "You're just like Nonna." I hear my voice bounce off the bare walls that should have some kind of wallpaper or sconces. "He said he wanted to be friends after the kiss. It makes me happy to be his friend. It makes me happy to kiss him. Why do you want me to be sad?"

"I don't want you to be sad. But these emotions you're feeling, they're new to you. You need a chance to get used to them before you start a romantic relationship." She reaches out to me, and her hand on mine feels funny.

A person's touch goes deeper than the warmth and pressure on the skin. It goes through the body to the heart and brain. Jennifer's hand on mine lets me know that she likes me.

A scratch begins in my throat and tears spill onto my cheeks. When I cry, my nose gets stuffy and runny at the same time. I hiccough. "I want to feel happy all the time. I don't want to feel this sadness."

"That's the problem with emotions. You can't get just the good ones." Jennifer's real smile returns. "You've made such remarkable progress. I never expected the results to be so drastic. Still, I think you need to be wary of a man who kisses a woman in your state."

"My state?"

"I just mean that he knows you have autism. He knows you don't understand emotions. I don't think his motives are as friendly as he says."

The heat returns to my head, but this time it's not tears that come to my face, but a blurry vision. Everything looks cloudy, and I can't hear well. I'm about to tell Jennifer that she has no idea about my state, that my autism is going away or at least I'm learning new emotions on top of it. I open my mouth, and Kyle walks in with Jerome.

"Group is going to start. We can talk more after." Jennifer greets the others.

I don't listen as they start going around the room trying to explain how they used social skills. All I can think about is how Jennifer is wrong. Chris doesn't have bad motives. Sarah is wrong. Chris doesn't want sex. And Nonna is wrong to keep me away from him because she doesn't like his family.

"That was a good story, Kyle. You did well. Even though you didn't have a conversation, you used the 'introduce yourself' skill very well."

"No he didn't," I say. "Every week you tell them about how they did the skills well. Every week it's the same thing. They don't get it. They're not improving on the medicine. Can't you see?" I wave my arms around to indicate the entire group.

"I'm giving positive feedback, because Kyle tried really hard. And everyone improves at their own pace. Gina, you're not being kind."

"I'm done being kind." I stand up. "I don't belong in here anymore. You lie, Jennifer, that's what you do."

I run from the room. I can't see in front of me, but I make it to the stairs. I won't wait for the elevator. I can barely get oxygen in my lungs. I burst out of the stairway and through the door onto the street.

It's an hour before Nonna will be waiting for me

at home. No one knows where I am or what I am going to do.

Even me.

CHRIS

I watch the progress across my computer screen. Our boys are buying Genloran left and right. I pump my fists in the air.

Next, the waiting game. As soon as Genloran is done with their phase three trials, the FDA will approve it, and wham. The stock price will jump. And once that crazy pill hits the market, the dough will come rolling in.

My desk phone rings.

"Mr. Rinaldi, you have a visitor in the lobby," the security guard informs me.

"A visitor?"

"A young woman, Gina?"

My mind tries to refocus away from the climbing stats. "Gina's here? Okay, send her up."

I push back from the desk and walk to the bank of elevators. My stomach shouldn't be getting butterflies at the thought of seeing Gina. She's just a friend, a pal.

A girl-buddy.

Since that kiss, I haven't been to any clubs in the city, and while in the Hamptons, I volunteered to be the designated driver each night.

The doors pull apart and Gina steps out. She wears a denim mini skirt and a black t-shirt that has a dusting of cocoa powder from the coffee shop over her left breast. Man, her tits are huge. She has the typical Italian hourglass shape that I usually don't go for. The leggy Manhattan blondes are more my taste.

Maybe it's her cascade of chestnut curls, maybe it's the high I feel from the Genloran sales, but a goofy smile spreads across my face when she nears me.

"Hey, Gina."

"Hi, Chris. I, uh…" She shifts her weight from side to side. "I had some time, and I wanted to see you."

"I want to see you too. Come, I'll show you my office." I motion for her to follow me. "It's not that impressive, but it's mine."

Heads turn as we walk down the hall. Rob nearly dislocates a vertebra in his neck trying to catch a glimpse.

"Here it is." A swell of pride still hits me when I show off my ten-by-twelve space.

Gina surveys the room, hands on her hips, and purses her lips.

She opens her mouth and clamps it shut.

"Spit it out, Gina. I know you want to say something about the room or the furniture."

She smiles, and her eyes actually get brighter. They turn from a deep green to a more gold color.

I've never seen anything like it.

"I was practicing being polite. Sometimes it's best to keep my opinions to myself."

"Not with me. I want you to be honest with me all the time. That's what I like about you."

She nods. "Then we need to move this desk, and what's the chance you can get a different visitor chair?"

After twenty minutes of grunting and shoving office furniture around a carpeted floor, I have to admit it looks better. My tiny room seems much bigger. "You're right about that chair. It does look too much like another desk chair. I'll see what I can request. Thanks."

She leans against the desk, and her skirt rides up. "Chris, you want me to be honest?"

"All the time."

"I like you, and I think I want to be your girlfriend." She looks right through me. "If you don't want to be my boyfriend, that would be okay. I'd be sad, but I'd still want to be your friend. Can we?"

A very unmanly squeak comes out of my throat. Then I laugh. "You know what?" I close the distance between us. "I think I'd like to try this boyfriend-girlfriend proposal of yours." I place my hands on her hips, taking in her soft flesh.

"I thought you would. Sarah thought so, too." Gina lifts her arms and holds them in midair.

"Now is when you put them around my neck," I

whisper in her ear.

"Another movie kiss?" she whispers back.

"Oh yeah."

And the kiss does seem like it belongs in a movie. Her tongue sweeps inside and tangles with mine. I press in between her legs, hiking her skirt all the way up. I know I have a glass wall that everyone can look through, I know she's never been kissed like this, but damn, none of that matters.

I pull back, coming to my senses. "Gina, I'm not sure you understand the whole boyfriend-girlfriend thing." I step away and she pulls her skirt down.

"Yes I do. We're going to go on dates and kiss more." She lowers her eyelids and grins. "And have sex. Only…let's wait a few dates before the sex?"

"Yeah, definitely a few dates before the sex." I rub my face to try to come back to reality. "Should I talk to your nonna?"

"I'll deal with Nonna." Gina walks to the door. "You'll have to call me now and ask me on a date."

"I will."

Her ass twitches as she walks away. I will never find a woman who talks as straightforwardly as she does, one who is as honest and sincere. No head games or jealousy.

Her innocence is a concern, but better me than some guy who doesn't know her, doesn't know where she comes from, or doesn't understand what she deals with.

GINA

"Sarah, this doesn't feel right." I wiggle into the cerulean-blue skirt that we bought at the discount store across the street. Inside the small bathroom of Perks Plus, I can't see what it looks like in the mirror above the sink. "It sticks to my legs." I tug at the side.

"Come out and let me see," Sarah calls from outside.

I twist the knob and try to stride out of the room, but the skirt constricts my movement.

"Are you kidding? It's perfect." Sarah circles around me. "And the white top is great, shows off your amazing hair color. Do you know how much some women pay to get your auburn color?"

"No, how much?"

She shakes her head. "No, it's one of those questions you don't answer."

I let out a sigh. "I don't feel comfortable."

"You're not supposed to." Sarah fluffs my hair. "Are you nervous?"

"I think so. I can't tell if I'm nervous about going on a date with Chris or walking in this skirt. At least you're letting me wear comfortable shoes."

"I couldn't convince you otherwise. You're going to have a blast. Remember, don't kiss him until the end of the date."

"Why?"

"It's just how it's done. And relax. I know that's a stupid thing to say. But you're funny when you relax. Funny in a good way. And you're smart, and interesting. Try to be all of those things."

I hold my head in my hands. "Sarah, I don't know how to be all of those things. I just am."

"And you're great." She pulls me into a hug. It's warm with her gripping me, but I don't squirm away because she needs to hug me now. "When I first agreed to take a worker from the Autism Center, I had no idea who they would send. I figured it would be someone who needed help with the routine work. But you picked all that up immediately." She releases me and her eyes are moist. "I never expected that I'd have to help with dating skills." She swipes at her eyes.

"Thanks for your help. Really, I do appreciate it." I step back into the bathroom to look at my face. "I like the makeup we picked out."

"It's much more natural."

"And I never expected to need help getting ready for a date. I like him. He's handsome and kind." I walk back to Sarah and hug her. I do it right this time, not too hard, and I don't pin her arms to her side. "It feels so wonderful to have a guy like Chris like me. Scary but wonderful."

The bell on the door chimes, and Chris walks into the half-dim coffee shop.

"I wasn't sure if you were open." He stops in his

tracks. "Wow, you look fantastic." The smile on his face is contagious, because I feel the corners of my mouth pull up. Also, he gets little dimples when he smiles, and that makes my belly flip.

"I'll lock up." Sarah takes a step toward Chris. "Where are you going?" There's an edge to her voice.

"Dinner and a comedy club. Is that okay?" Chris is looking at Sarah instead of me. "And I'll put her in a cab home."

"I'm right here." I wave my arms. "Sarah, Chris is a good guy. He's already said we won't have sex for a while." I grab my bag and join him by the door.

Sarah laughs and Chris's face has gone beet red.

"Are we going on our first real date?" I tug at his arm.

He clears his throat. And when he turns to look at me, his color returns to normal and his eyes seem to look inside me and see my thoughts. "I've been looking forward to it all week."

Chapter 9

CHRIS

Walking arm in arm with Gina is awkward because of our height difference. But her delicate elbow pressing into my side is the nicest discomfort.

"I thought we'd go to a Thai restaurant. Do you like Thai food?"

"I don't know. We'll find out. If I don't, I'll eat something else later." She scans the stores as we walk past.

I can't help the guffaw that comes out.

"Oops. I don't think I was supposed to say that aloud. It wasn't very polite." She turns her questioning green eyes up at me, and I want to erase her doubt.

"No, it wasn't polite, but it was honest. And I'd rather you be honest. It's what I like about you."

"It's what I like about you, too, Chris." She leans into me so her head rests on my arm. It's not the most natural time for her to do this, and I worry that her head will bump along as we walk, but she's trying it out and I enjoy the contact. "From the beginning you've been very open with me.

Straightforward about why you asked me to the party. It makes it easy to be with you."

I can't respond, because honesty has never been my strong suit. And certainly not a quality I cultivate in my life.

"We're here."

I open the door for her, and she pauses to adjust to the change of lighting. She scrutinizes every corner of the room, taking mental notes of the décor and design.

At the table, she reads each item on the menu. I have to ask the waitress to come back because Gina is only on page two.

"Do you like spicy foods?" I ask.

"I guess. Nonna makes arrabbiata sauce."

"Most of this stuff is a little spicier than that. But there are some that aren't."

She slaps the menu closed with enough force to attract the attention of the diners at the next table.

"You order for me," she says. "That's a romantic thing to do on a date."

"You make this too easy for me, Gina." I order a few dishes, hoping she'll at least like the noodles, and a glass of wine for myself.

"I'd like a ginger ale, please," Gina says quietly.

I'm sure she doesn't have much experience with alcohol, and I'm relieved she doesn't want to start tonight. Maybe in the past, I wanted a girl to be a little tipsy to make my job easier. But Gina is an open book, and there's no plan to turn her pages tonight.

The conversation is much more natural than I thought it would be. She shares all the things that are wrong with the design of the restaurant. And I am sincerely interested. It's not some boring girl thing about colors—there are actual reasons behind her criticism.

And she's brilliant about the market and financial subjects. A girl who reads the business section is a very sexy thing.

"So you like the food," I say as she heaps more of the spicy basil dish on her plate.

"My mouth is on fire, but I love it." The forkful passes over her lips and I watch as she chews. Her eyes open. She must have bitten down on a pepper. "Whoa. Hot." She gulps her drink and settles into her seat. "This is fun."

I lean across the table and cover her lips with mine. She doesn't respond, so I pull back.

"Sorry." I sit back and focus on my plate. That was a rookie mistake on my part.

"Sarah said not to kiss until the end of the date," she whispers.

"Why?"

"I don't know." She reaches out and takes my hand. "Do we have to wait?"

"I won't tell Sarah if you don't." I place my hand on her soft cheek and bring her face close to mine.

The kiss is laced with spicy food and sticky-sweet ginger ale. But her passion overwhelms me. It doesn't matter that we're in a restaurant. We might as well be in a bedroom. Her mouth really is on fire.

When she sits back, a smug, satisfied expression rests on her face. "I'm going to tell Sarah anyway."

We laugh and finish our meal.

We kiss on and off as we walk to the comedy club. We don't talk much, but the silence is comfortable.

Inside, Gina gives me the rundown on the dimensions of the space and how they could probably fit more tables in if they altered it.

The waitress is about to give me a hard time about ginger ales not counting toward the two-drink minimum when I glare at her and promise to make it up in her tip if she can find it in her heart to bring us what we order.

"You weren't very kind to her," Gina says.

"She wasn't kind to us."

"No, she wasn't kind to me. And you intervened." She looks into the distance. "It's okay, that's what friends do — they stick up for each other."

"I'll stick up for you, Gina." I rub her shoulder.

"I know. And if I can ever return the favor, I will." She leans into me for one more kiss before the emcee takes the stage.

I watch Gina more than the acts. When she laughs, it's with her whole body. And I'm not just eyeing her tits when she moves. It's the veins in her neck, the flush of her face, and the spreading of her lips across her teeth.

Ugh, it's going to be a few months full of cold showers. Because Gina is right—I'll watch out for her.

GINA

Nonna is praying the rosary. She does this every time I get ready for a date.

"When will you be back, Gina *mia*?" She looks older than I have ever seen her before.

My chest hurts, and it's hard to swallow. "I don't know. Do I have a curfew?" I've learned sarcasm, and it feels both good and bad to use it.

"No." She shakes her head. "You've been out three times this week. Do you have to see so much of the Rinaldi boy?"

"Only twice with Chris. Sarah had a party at her house one night." I flop on the couch next to her. "I thought you wanted me to have friends."

"I do…" She smiles, and a bit of the spark that is Nonna returns. "I never expected for it to really happen. I'm trying very hard, Gina *mia*, to find happiness for you. I worry." She drops her beads in her lap.

"Jennifer is having a hard time getting used to it, too. It's been two weeks since my last set of tests, and she still can't believe the progress I've made. She also doesn't trust Chris. But he's been so much fun."

"It is a miracle drug." Nonna pats my knee. "Or just a miracle. It's what we always wanted for you. I thought you'd never grow up, and here you are. It gives me some comfort knowing you'll be okay when I'm gone."

"Stop talking like that. You're healthy as a horse. See that? I used another idiom. I'm really great at that now." I kiss the papery skin on her cheek. She smells of lavender soap, and I go back to that day I moved in with her. "Momma left because she couldn't handle taking care of an autistic kid, didn't she?"

"Your mother loved you." Nonna repeats this in the same robotic tone she always uses, but only now do I realize it's what she has practiced saying instead of the truth.

"I don't have the emotional memories, but I know she got fed up with me. Was that it? She couldn't stand the fact that I had stopped learning?"

Nonna bends her head to hide the tears, and she clasps the rosary in her cracked hands. "Some things are best left in the past. Especially now that…"

"Now that what?" There is a reason my mother left. Something more than just the fact that she couldn't watch my stagnant progress.

A knock on the door.

"That Rinaldi boy is here." Nonna stands and smooths her housedress. She crosses to the door, but

I'm stuck on the couch.

I hear Nonna greet Chris, but I can't take my eyes off the spot where she just sat.

"You okay?" Chris dwarfs Nonna. He's just shy of six feet, and Nonna can only reach five in her clunky black shoes.

He's wearing a linen jacket over a black t-shirt. I admire his chest muscles and the jeans that sit on his narrow hips. He chuckles. I haven't gotten good at looking at his body without being obvious yet. I've seen Sarah "check out" a guy from her peripheral vision and by flipping her hair back so she can give him a quick glance. I need to practice that.

"Yeah, I'm fine." I stand and grab my purse.

"We'll be home by one," Chris assures Nonna.

She is stiffly holding the colorful bouquet he brought her. Chris has tried a bakery box of cookies and a bottle of expensive perfume. It doesn't look like the flowers will soften her up either, but it's nice that he tries.

"She doesn't have a curfew." Nonna mimics my sarcasm and clomps into the kitchen.

Nonna might be worried about me, but I'm worried about her.

CHRIS

The club thumps with music pouring out of every corner. I have my hand on the small of Gina's back to guide her. She stiffens against it.

"Are you sure you want to be here?" My lips press against her ear.

She nods. "I want to hang out with you and your friends."

I cock my head to the side and steer her to my usual corner. Rob sprawls on the couch with a girl on each side. I bump fists hello to him and to a few other traders there. It's quieter in this spot, and we have easy eye contact with the cocktail waitresses at the end of the bar.

"This is Gina." I sit on the edge of the couch and pull Gina to perch on my knee.

She fits comfortably there, and my hand around her hips lets everyone know I won't be interested in anyone else tonight.

What a relaxed feeling, not having to flirt or be on the make.

I have a date and no need to scope out any other girl. Plus, this girl is hot. In the past few weeks, Gina has taken to reading fashion magazines in addition to her usual furniture catalogues. She's on a budget, but puts together some smoking outfits.

I've told her we'll go slowly, and I am happy to give my libido a break. But her tiny black skirt rides up so high that I can feel the heat from between her legs against my lap.

"How'd the day end for you?" I ask Rob.

"Two hundred up." He lifts his martini in a

salute.

I shake my head. "I don't know how you do it."

"You don't want to know how he does it," another trader says.

Gina looks at me with a furrowed brow, and I shake my head. She's gotten good at stopping herself from asking questions that would show she's out of touch. I don't really mind when we're alone, but with other people it's a little embarrassing. And she's great about not wanting to embarrass me or herself.

The waitress comes over, and I order a martini.

"I'll have a Diet Coke." Gina has also learned that girls can drink diet soda, but not ginger ale or orange juice.

"Gina, I love your top. Where'd you get it?" The girl on Rob's right runs her finger around the rim of her mojito and licks it.

"A thrift store in Queens." Gina's honesty makes me shift in my seat. The expression on the girl's face freezes, but it doesn't matter. I laugh. Her opinion of Gina doesn't matter. Rob's opinion doesn't matter. I like Gina, and we have fun together.

She doesn't participate much in the conversation. Instead, she gulps her drink and takes everything in. She's probably never been to a club before, at least not a real NYC club, and the lights and crush of bodies might be overwhelming. But I can tell she's taking notes for future use, like an anthropologist studying New Yorkers in their native habitat.

There's not much conversation anyway. Although I'm the most educated guy, I prefer to hang with the traders rather than the other analysts. I left Queens, but part of me will always identify with the working guy, the low man on the totem pole. I might want the VP spot, and might even get it, but will I ever fit into it?

"Can we dance?" Gina interrupts and gives a little burp, her empty Coke glass showing that she has finished it off.

"Dance?"

"I know how." She huffs.

I raise her off my lap and lead her to the dance floor. It's packed with writhing bodies.

"So, how did you learn to dance?" I've pulled her against me, the length of her body impressed on me, and we're not dancing, just swaying as the energy of the masses influences us.

"YouTube videos." She smiles, steps back, and shows me what she's got.

Her arms are above her head, and her hips swivel. Damn, I have to keep my cool so I don't get hard. I hold her hips and mirror her moves.

She's got it all, from the lazy, sexy smile, to the just-right amount of jiggle in her tits. I forget everything stressful—my job, my family that's been demanding another visit, the bitchy girl sitting with Rob—everything.

All that exists is Gina, her mass of curly hair shimmering under the dizzying lights, her hot bod, and the smile she's got just for me.

Then she stops and her face contorts into fear.

I stutter-step to her. "What is it?"

"Diet Coke makes me have to pee." She panic-scans the room.

"Over there." I point to the corner.

She nods and weaves between the swarm.

I turn to head back to my group and come face-to-face with bitch girl.

"Don't you remember me, Chris?" She teeters a little on her five-inch platforms with ribbons that wrap up her calves. There isn't another bit of fabric on her incredible legs until just below her crotch. Where a strap of spandex serves as a skirt.

"Of course I do." I frantically roll through my brain. I'm sure I did her one night, but when, and what was her name?

"I'm a little insulted you didn't say anything when you came in." She snakes her arms around my neck and draws me in. Her breath is laced with rum.

"I'm with someone." I nod toward the bathrooms.

"Come on, Chris. She's got no style. Secondhand clothes and diet soda? She didn't take one look at you while she sat on your lap. But looked everywhere else." She stretches to my ear. "Do you know what I would do if I sat on your lap?"

"I've got a pretty good idea." I put my hands on her waist to push her back.

"Christopher?" Gina's voice is small, but it cuts me.

I've never seen sadness in her face. It isn't anger. It's pain. And the panic returns to her eyes.

"Bye." I push away from the girl and take Gina's hand. I half drag her outside. The warm summer air is moist but refreshing after the crush of bodies. "Gina, I didn't want to touch her. You have to believe me. She came on to me." I've never pleaded with a woman before. I've never wanted one to forgive me for something before.

Tears run down her face, and her drugstore makeup can't withstand it. She's sobbing now and can't catch her breath. A cab stops in front of the club. When the passengers spill out, I whisk her in.

"We're headed to Rego Park." I smooth Gina's hair as I bark at the driver.

"You gotta be kidding me. How am I going to earn a fare back from Queens?" The driver turns around.

"I'm headed back to the city after we drop my date off," I growl.

The cabbie hits the meter, and we pull away from the curb.

"You believe me, right?" Desperation jerks at my heart. I have no experience comforting women, and even less comforting autistic women.

"I-I believe y-you." The gasps are subsiding. "When I saw her hand on you, I...I got angry and sad at the same time." Gina's back to her wonderment phase, which amazes me. I love seeing emotions through the naiveté of her eyes.

"I didn't want to make you jealous. She's an old girlfriend." I'm not about to explain my string of one-night stands to her.

"You were her boyfriend?"

"Not really..."

"You just had sex with her." Gina's no-nonsense self is returning.

I laugh. "Yeah, sorry."

"Why? It was before we were dating." She's stopped crying, and accepts my hand when I offer it. The streets of Midtown overflow with cars and pedestrians. Broadway shows are just letting out, and we inch along to the East Side. Her hand feels good in mine. She looks out the window, and I can almost hear the gears turning. "Is sex is as good as it seems in movies and books?"

Heat rushes to my face. "What movies have you been watching?"

"I've seen some porn on the internet. There are some videos that are instructional. Nonna won't discuss it with me. I've also checked some books out of the library. Did you know there's an entire self-help section on sex?"

"The public library would be the last place I

would think to look for help in that area. But it's probably better than anything your nonna might share with you." I tap my fingers against the seat and take a deep breath. "Yeah, sex is good. But it can also be..." I run my finger across her palm. She shivers. "It feels good, but it feels better when you really like the person. Because you want to make that person feel as good as you feel." I sigh. "That doesn't make sense."

"Yes it does." She leans into me, and we kiss.

It's an amazing kiss. Her hand strokes my cheek and I entwine my fingers in her hair.

She doesn't break the kiss, but takes one of my hands and places it on her shirt. There is no way I can take her breast in one hand. She more than fills it. I ease her shirt up and under her bra and rub her nipple.

"Oooh," she squeals. Her eyes flash to the driver, who has decided to turn the volume of the radio up high. She nods eagerly. "More of that."

We make out like teenagers in the back of the cab all the way through the Midtown Tunnel. I even run my hand up her skirt and massage her through her panties. I don't dare go under the panties in a cab. Gina's never had this before, and a taxi is not the place to introduce her to finger fucking.

"I think I'll like sex when we do it." She leans her head against my chest, and I'm going to need a frigid shower tonight.

Chapter 10

GINA

"Nonna, do we have my high school diploma around here?" I rifle through the file cabinet in the kitchen. It's neatly filled with every card or picture I ever made. I pull out a birthday card I made when I was in fourth grade. The letters are precisely aligned in blue crayon. I drew a heart and a star in perfect symmetry. Even as a kid I could see how to divide space. It occurs to me that I never drew a person. I doubt I could get past a stick figure. I smile inside, realizing it would be a perfectly proportional stick figure.

One folder has all the papers that show Nonna is my conservator. She became my guardian right after my mother left. I was almost eighteen and a legal adult. But even after I turned eighteen, I still needed someone to take care of me. I understood nothing about how to get along in the world.

"What do you need your diploma for?"

"My application to Reynolds School for Interior Design." I stand up with the folder in my hand.

"How long are you going to be my conservator?"

Nonna snatches the folder from me and replaces it in the drawer. She dips her hand into a folder in the back. "Here's your diploma."

This is one of those situations Jennifer has talked about. When people change the subject and act angry, it means they don't want to answer your question. I stand a little taller with this knowledge. Sometimes you have to plan to ask the question another time. Pick and choose your battles. And right now I need to fight my way into college.

"I'm going to the drugstore to scan this. Then all I need is a ninety-five-dollar check for the application fee."

"Ninety-five dollars!" Nonna puts her hands on her hips.

I roll my eyes. "I have the money. I'll give it to you so you can write the check." I go into my purse. "Maybe I should get my own checking account."

"No, no. I'll take care of it." She sits down at the kitchen table and puts on her reading glasses to write the check.

I take the seat across from her. We've sat here countless times, having meals, doing puzzles. But it seems foreign now. There's a purpose to why I want to sit with her. And it's my purpose.

"Aren't you happy for me?"

"Why shouldn't I be?" She doesn't meet my eyes.

Nonna has been so used to caring for me. She might lose that role soon. When a realization like this springs into my mind, I'm amazed that I can understand it.

"I've changed. It's hard for you to get used to how I've changed. I have my own ideas and plans. I have friends—"

She snorts. "Friends. All I see is the Rinaldi boy coming around for you. If taking medicine means you're going to keep company with that type of person, then maybe you shouldn't take it no more."

Icy-sharp pain tears in my chest. The balloon fizzles out, and instead I grow small. "Nonna?"

"Bah! I don't mean it." She rips the check from the book and slaps it on the table in front of me. "You should have a way to support yourself when I'm gone. A decorator is as good as any."

"Interior design." I slide the check into the envelope. "If I change then you have to change, too. You can't treat me like how I was. I understand things now. I know exactly what Chris wants in a girlfriend. And I'm going to be that girlfriend." I pause as the color drains out of Nonna's face, but it doesn't stop me. I stand and grab my purse. "I'm going to be like all other women my age. I'm going to have a career, friends, a boyfriend, and sex."

Nonna crosses herself.

I've hurt her by saying these things, but I can't unsay them.

Tears spring up in my eyes, and I swipe them away. "I hate crying all the time." I storm out of the house and allow the front door to rattle in the frame.

Those pills come with warnings of nausea and dry mouth. But they don't tell you about the side effects of emotions.

CHRIS

"I can't believe you're leaving early." Rob adjusts his sunglasses and lies back in the deck chair. "It's our last weekend."

The timeshare started as a blast, but as I've been seeing more and more of Gina, I can't seem to get into the spirit of things. "It's my dad's birthday party. I've got to meet them at the house when they get back from church." I gather my still-damp beach towel and shove it in my duffel.

He twists his head to the side. "You haven't been much fun since you started dating Gina, anyway. But I will miss having you as a designated driver."

"It's Sunday. Try not to drink too much." I fist-bump him.

"Bro, it's Sunday. Bloody Marys are in order. See you tomorrow at the factory."

I hoof it into town to catch the LIRR back to Jamaica, Queens. I'll get a taxi from there. Rob is correct—I haven't been much fun lately. At least not with him. The train rattles along and I replay my last date with Gina at Coney Island.

She'd been before, but she said she'd never enjoyed it as much. Watching her discover each new emotion, each new experience, brought me a joy I never thought I'd feel again. Since Carina's death, I had given up on joy. My plan was keep my head down, earn a buttload of money, spend it, and then...I had no plans past then.

I deserve every minute of misery I have. Leaving my little sister alone in the community pool is a sin I will never be absolved of.

But walking along with Gina as she wakes up to a new world wakes me up to a new world as well. It gives me a glimpse of what life is like for a person without a black mark on their soul. For a normal person.

I chuckle. A woman with autism is the one to show me what normal is. How fucked up am I?

The taxi pulls up to the curb of my family's ranch house. A few cousins are sitting on the lawn. I pay and drag my bag out, along with the gift I've gotten for Pop.

I greet everyone, and it takes five minutes to work my way to the kitchen, where I find Momma.

"Christofo, you're here." Her eyes widen but she doesn't stop stirring the gravy. It's got to be ninety-five degrees outside, but that won't stop Mother Rinaldi from making a proper Sunday dinner, full of wonderful carbs.

"I said I'd come." I peck her on the cheek and get a brief smile.

"Go find your brother and father." She points with her spoon to the back.

I find Pop sitting with Marco. The television is tuned to the Mets game, and now is the perfect time to give Pop his gift.

"Hey, Marco. Hi, Pop." I punch my brother in the arm and place a kiss on my father's cheek.

Marco responds with a slap on my back. Pop doesn't react.

"What's the score?" I sit next to Pop on the wicker couch.

"Mets are down by five, bottom of the seventh."

"Wait till next year." I unzip my bag and pull out a blue plastic three-ring binder. "Pop, here's your birthday gift." I hold it out to him.

He takes his eyes off the screen and looks down at it. After a moment, he reaches out and strokes it.

"Go on, open it." I wiggle it like I'm luring in a fish with shiny bait.

He takes it and opens the cover.

"Whoa." Marco looks over Pop's shoulder. "Is that all the cards?"

"Yep, every card of every Met player from '86."

My father is a lifelong Mets fan, and one of the happiest moments of his life was going to Game 2 of the 1986 World Series. I hadn't been born yet, but my older siblings vaguely recall the day. Dad worked for the sanitation department and won employee of the year. His prize was two tickets. He took his brother, Uncle Joe, and despite the unusually cold October night, they proudly wore their short-sleeve Gary Carter jerseys.

He flips through the pages of the baseball cards, carefully reviewing each one. He nods. The faintest of smiles tugs at the corners of his mouth.

Marco's jaw drops open, and he looks at me. My breath catches in my chest.

"The Keith Hernandez one is bent at the corner," Pop rasps.

Marco laughs and I let out a breath. "Yeah, Pop. It was hard to find a good one."

Pop looks up at me. For a nanosecond we lock eyes and I see the man who taught me to hold a Louisville Slugger, the man who scolded me when I broke Momma's glass figurine with that same bat, and the man who taught us all to look out for each other. He taught us that siblings stood up for one another, no matter if we were wrong. If one of my brothers (or sisters) got into a neighborhood fight, we all turned up to share in the action. We protected each other.

I remember how I let him down by failing in my brotherly tasks.

The moment passes, and the veil comes down over his eyes again. He returns a blank stare to the television.

Marco discreetly wipes a tear from his eye and coughs to cover a sob.

"Why are you watching that depressing game? Come sit down to eat," Momma commands from the hall.

Marco and I help Pop get to his feet. He is still strong, just stiff from sitting in one spot all day. At only sixty-two, he could still work, if his mind hadn't left him.

The usual commotion of a Sunday dinner happens. There's never time to take more than two bites of food before you find a dish being passed down your side of the table. I learned early that you'd better take a spoonful of whatever it was, because the bowl was not likely to make its way back to you. Unless it was spinach. That always made the rounds plenty of times.

"I don't care what they say, I'm not going to Saint John's," Momma proclaims, and clatters her fork against the dish.

Vicki answers my enquiring look. "The archdiocese wants to merge our parishes. Not enough priests, not enough parishioners." She shrugs.

"Humph." Momma drums her fingers on the table. "There are Puerto Ricans at Saint John's."

"Jesus loves all people," I say through a mouthful of macaroni.

I earn one of Momma's dagger-throwing stares.

I shift—not because of the stare, I'm used to those. But my phone has been vibrating the hell out of my butt for a few minutes. I decide it's time to check.

There are two missed calls and three texts from Gina. I keep my phone in my lap and check the texts.

I got into design school!!!!!!

"Yes." I pump my fist in the air.

All conversation stops at my outburst. A sea of familiar and similar faces turns to me. Each of my siblings and their respective kids have inherited Momma's green eyes and Pop's Roman nose. It's like a genetic study around the table.

"Well?" Momma holds out her hands.

"Gina Giancarlo was accepted to Reynolds School of Design. She's going to be an interior designer."

"Why is she calling you?" Momma asks in a choked voice.

"We've become friends. She works near me, and we've been hanging out."

"Hanging out?" Vicki's eyebrows disappear under her bangs.

"Seeing each other, a bit." I take a deep breath. "Why do you all dislike her so much? She's changed a lot. She understands things now. She's normal. What have you got against her?"

Momma pushes back her chair and walks into the kitchen. The kids are shooed away with promises of dessert if they go outside to play.

The chicken sits like a lump in my gut. Something has happened.

"You ran off after Carina…" Marco starts.

"What?"

"Gina Giancarlo is the reason Carina drowned." Rico's voice is barely audible.

"No, she wasn't." I stand, and my Coke topples over into my plate. Foaming soda pools around the pasta.

"Chris, she was the one last seen playing with Carina. She said —"

"No. I was. I was supposed to keep an eye on her. Momma…Momma left me in charge of her." I try to breathe to steady my voice, but oxygen won't come in. Nothing comes in.

"You left right after. You never heard that part of the story," Donny says.

"Carina wanted her towel. She left it under the trees." My head throbs. "I went to get it. The sky darkened and the lifeguard blew his whistle. It was going to rain. It was…"

"The storm came fast," Marco agrees.

"Everyone was running. Everywhere." I grip the back of my chair but still my body shakes. "I couldn't find her. The lifeguard said everyone was out of the pool. I thought…I thought she went home with one of you."

"Chris, it wasn't your fault. Gina was playing

with Carina and —"

"No." I twist, throwing the chair to the floor.

I walk out without thinking of where I am going.

I walk. I can remember Gina that day, but she was a different person than she is today. I can hardly reconcile the two people. Back then Gina never smiled, never talked above a monotone, never made eye contact. But that didn't make her dangerous. Certainly not intentionally dangerous.

Could it be that she was somehow guilty without meaning to be?

No, it was still my fault. I was responsible for my baby sister, and I didn't look for her. The lifeguard said the pools were empty, and I believed him. It wasn't until we were all back at the house that we realized Carina was missing. And it wasn't until the rain stopped that they found her lifeless body in the pool.

Cars honk at me as I cross the street without stopping. The afternoon August air hangs heavy, laden with barbecue, cut grass, and the garbage waiting at the curb for Monday's trucks.

Little Carina, a surprise to everyone, especially my father. I had been the baby of the family for ten years. A devout Catholic, my mother had all of us kids so close together. My best guess is that she kicked Pop out of the bed for a few years until she thought it was safe for him to return without any more babies.

But even if Carina wasn't expected, she was loved. She didn't just have parents, she had all of us as protectors. It made her a little spoiled, but we didn't mind. She was our little *princessa*, and her love of gymnastics meant one of us was always walking her to or from practice. She got special classes even if the rest of us just got thrown into whatever sport was offered at the community center.

Gina lived a few houses down, and always played with the younger kids. That was where she fit. But not now. Now she was headed to college, and she was going to have a career.

How much has her mind changed? Can she remember that day? And if she can, can she remember it as she was then?

I walk for about an hour before I realize I'm in Rego Park. A mere six blocks from her house. I could ask her. I could maybe finally discover the truth of that day.

Chapter 11

GINA

"Naughty Girl" blares from the speakers. This song was popular when I was in high school, and I memorized all the lyrics. But dancing to it now in the living room, I feel all the energy of the rhythm; the melody flows through my arms as I wave them over my head.

Nonna would never let me play music this loud. But she's visiting Great-Aunt Carolina and won't be back for hours.

I didn't call her with the news. When I opened the email, I jumped in the air, knocking my Diet Coke over. I'm developing a taste for that. Then I texted Chris and Sarah—my two friends. I also sent an email to Jennifer. But Nonna I will have to tell in person. I want to see her face beam with pride.

A loud knock startles me, and I trip over the refinished coffee table.

"Ouch." I rub my shin on my way to the door. I peep through the curtain, and Chris is on the top step.

I fling the door open and grab him in a hug that

nearly sends us both flying down the stoop.

"I got in," I squeal in his ear.

"Okay, okay." His back is damp from sweat and his black hair is plastered to his forehead. His buttoned shirt tapers along the lines of his waist and disappears into a pair of chinos sitting low on his hips, but not hiding his tight buns, which I grab. "Tight buns" is a phrase I've always understood. But now I have a new appreciation for it.

"Hey, not in front of the neighbors." He gently pushes me back inside and shuts the door behind him. "Where's your nonna?" His usual grin is missing.

"She's at her sister's." I pick up my soda. "Aren't you going to congratulate me?"

He steps past me to sit on the couch. "Huh?"

"Didn't you get my text? I got into Reynolds." I jump on the couch next to him, causing him to bounce. "That's why you're here, right? Weren't you just at your father's birthday party?"

"My father's birthday." He rakes his hand through his hair and it stands on end, but I still want to kiss him.

I slide close to him. "Something's bothering you." It feels wonderful to be able to pick up on the clues—his distracted manner, the way he rubs his face.

He looks at me, his eyes piercing, and I squirm away an inch. Then his face relaxes and his grin returns. "Tell me about Reynolds."

Something is still in the back of his mind, but I'm too excited to try to decipher the code of facial expressions and tone of voice. Right now, I'm filling my balloon up with air, pumped with pride and excitement.

"Look at the welcome video they sent." I turn my laptop to face him and hit play for the fourteenth time.

Chris watches the video and turns his gorgeous eyes to me. "I'm happy for you. This is very exciting."

"I'm nervous. Not anxious like I used to get, but nervous about the work, the other students…"

"You're going to do great. Look at this place." He waves his arm around the room. I have to admit, I did a great job with the small space. Getting rid of Nonna's big floral curtains and using a sheer drape makes the room seem bigger.

I lean in for a kiss, and he cradles my head in his hand. I love kissing him. A swarm of butterflies tickle me from the inside, and I get damp between my legs.

"I've decided I'm ready to have sex," I say when he pulls back.

"We will." He kisses my ear and strokes my breast through my shirt.

"Now. I've read all the books I can get. I have condoms in my room." I stand and pull his arm toward the steps.

He stands and brings me close. His kiss is fierce, and he's never been anything but super gentle with me. But now I feel his strength, and I want to feel the hard planes of his body against me. I want it to hurt just a little, to know that he's not treating me differently than any other woman he's ever had sex with.

I lead the way upstairs, his hand on my lower back urging me on. As if I'd back out now.

"I bought four different kinds because I didn't know which ones were right." I pull out four boxes of condoms, each with a different description. "Is ribbed better?" I ask, holding up a box.

He doesn't speak, but guides me to lie down. He hovers over me, and before I have time to feel nervous, we start kissing. It's like the other times we made out, only now he pulls my shirt completely off, rather than just hiking it up. My bra disappears pretty fast. But I take my time undoing his buttons. I want to see each inch of his skin revealed. I guess I was taking too long, because he rips it open and tears his undershirt off.

I've seen bare-chested men at the beach and on TV, but having one so close, the heat from his body hits mine even from inches away. I pull him on top of me. The crush feels good, and my nipples rub against his coarse hair.

He rolls me on top and takes my breast in his

mouth. I saw this in a porn movie and thought it looked weird, but man, does it feel good. Jolts of electricity zip around my body and I lose any clear thought. Which is good, because if my brain was online while he stripped my shorts off, I might be scared.

He looks into my eyes before he undoes his belt. I can read these clues. He's letting me know that once his pants are off, there's no turning back.

I nod vigorously and bite my lip. He chuckles, and I watch him wriggle out of his pants, taking his boxers down as well.

An erect penis is a funny thing. Frightening and enticing at the same time.

A giggle escapes me.

"You're not supposed to laugh," he grumbles in a teasing way.

"Then make me be serious."

"Mmmmm." He covers my mouth with his and his fingers slide down my belly. I know he's headed down there, but when he does massage my clit with his thumb, I'm surprised. Chris touches a place no one but me has ever touched, and I melt into my mattress.

Numbers that always hover in my mind vanish. With firm circles he's bringing me to an orgasm. I buck my hips and call his name. And he stops.

"What?" I open my eyes to see a wicked grin.

"It's part of the game," he rumbles.

So I turn on my side and wind my hand through the line of wiry hair that leads to his erection.

I expect it to be hard, like a rock, like I've read. But there's a hot, soft skin that moves with my palm, and I grip him.

"Like this." He covers my hand with his and I get the pumping action.

A bead of cum forms at the tip. My brain makes no decision. My body leads my mouth to cover the head, and it tastes salty and warm.

"Gina," he gasps, and raises his hips up to meet my mouth.

Just when I get the hang of it, he pulls away.

"Is sex all about teasing?" I ask.

He rolls me on my back and grabs a condom. It's not the ribbed kind.

"Yes, until the end. Then it's all about satisfaction."

He tears open the package and unrolls the condom over him.

A surge of icy panic slams into my gut. I am about to lose my virginity. Nonna and her rosary flash in my mind. But Chris has climbed between my legs, and all I see is his strong jaw, kind eyes, and lips I want to nibble on.

"Okay?" he asks. I could stop him, but why would I want to?

"Please." I want to add *be gentle*. But I don't, because I want to be as good as the girls from the city.

At first there's no pain, then a pinch like a needle at the doctor's. And after he has stroked me a few times from the inside, I allow my legs to fall open, and the friction is astonishing.

I keep my eyes open to watch him thrust into me. I meet his thrusts and wrap my legs around him.

He balances on one arm, and uses his thumb against my clit. The pressure builds and I lose my breath. The world spins. I dig my fingers into his back and hear my voice echo off the walls of my room.

I wilt for a moment. But he removes his hand to brace himself on either side of my head.

"You're so hot and tight." His face screws up as if he's in pain. His final thrusts are wild, and there's no way I can match the crazy pace. He's lost the easy rhythm he had before, and instead of his normally controlled self, he's become a bit wild.

I hold him tight and grit my teeth against the soreness. But when he cries my name, flushes, and throws his head back, it's all worth it.

He pants, rolls over, and takes me with him so we are nose to nose.

"You okay?" He kisses my cheek.

"Yeah. I liked it. I'm a little sore, though."

"Sorry about that. I should have been more careful."

"Nuh-uh." I kiss him. "I want to be like all the

other girls you've been with."

His eyes flash open and he caresses my hair. "Please don't ever be like the other girls."

CHRIS

I just deflowered Gina Giancarlo, the woman who possibly drowned my baby sister.

What was I thinking?

That's the problem: my brain has short-circuited.

That long, sweltering walk from my parents' house to here, I burned with determination to discover the truth of that day. For years my script had been that I was negligent and Carina died.

But everyone else seemed to think differently. I always assumed everyone knew, and that's why they treated me with such coldness. But it had been *me* who started the deep freeze.

Freshman orientation at SUNY Binghamton was scheduled for a week after she died. I packed my bags, got on a bus, and found a cheap motel to stay in until campus opened up. I hadn't come home for Thanksgiving, and when the dorms closed for winter break, the damage had already been done.

"You're sorry we did it." Gina's soft voice startles me.

"Not at all, baby." I run my fingers through her curls and along her delicate ear. "Just wondering if you are."

"Not at all." She bounds up, and her full breasts jiggle in a way that might make me want to start all over again. "That was so much fun. When can we do it again?"

I slide to sit up and rest my head against an uncomfortable iron headboard she must have rescued from a junk shop. "Normally, I'd need less than an hour, but I don't trust your nonna to be gone for that long."

"You're probably right." She sighs. "Can I watch you get dressed?"

"Only if I can watch you."

She giggles. A reverse striptease is more agonizing than a forward one. An ache forms as her breasts are covered by a plain white bra with a small flower in the middle. Matching panties slide over her hips and cover the mound of smaller chestnut curls. She's a natural.

It's my turn, and I exaggerate all my movements and hum a bump-and-grind beat.

She laughs so hard that she's no longer watching. It's infectious, and I sit next to her on the bed.

"Next time it won't hurt so much, and I'll go slower." I pull her close and kiss the tip of her nose.

"I don't mind. I'm glad it was you, Chris." She looks at me, and her gaze strikes me right through to my heart. "I can't imagine a better friend to do this with."

"We're more than friends, Gina." I shouldn't feel this budding love for anyone, especially her. But I can't kill it with my usual indifference. "I hope you feel that way, too." Why do my words sound like I'm being strangled?

"I do. I really feel it all."

"It's late. I'll call you later, and you can come by my office tomorrow. We'll have dinner in the city."

She takes my hand and walks me downstairs. I lean in to kiss her good-bye. This kiss is going to hold all the promise I want to be able to make to her, to myself. No matter the truth, we'll face it together.

The key turns in the front door.

"Nonna, you're back." Gina sidles away, and the chasm between us squeezes my heart.

"Of course I'm back. Did you expect me to move in with my sister?" She might be talking to Gina, but her stare is one hundred percent on me. Message received.

"I should be going." I peck Gina on the cheek, because Nonna might be in charge of this house, but Gina is mine.

Nonna's eyes never leave me as I cross to the door. "See you tomorrow. *Cara Mia, must we part? Each time we say good-bye my heart wants to die…*" I croon the oldie as I back down the steps.

Gina smiles behind her scowling grandmother. The door slams in my face, but I skip down the street.

I came here searching for answers, and I ended

up not wanting to know. The past is gone. I'm a different person now, and Gina is certainly a different person.

Instead of burying myself in booze and women, I'll redeem my lost years with the one woman who needs salvation most.

Chapter 12

GINA

The fluttering in my belly won't stop.

Not even Nonna's glower will tamp it down.

"What was he doing here? In my house."

I don't answer, because Nonna doesn't want to know. There are some questions people ask that they don't really want answered.

"Nonna, come look at this. I got into Reynolds, and they sent this cool video."

The frown disappears for a moment. "Good. I'm proud you'll be a college student." She joins me on the couch and watches over my shoulder.

I don't think I'll ever get tired of watching the students say welcome, or the corny greeting from the dean.

A true smile lights Nonna's face. "Gina *mia*, you've turned into a real young woman."

"In more ways than one." It slips out without my meaning it to.

Here's the problem with emotions: They make you do things without thinking.

You can be so filled up with excitement that it

stops your frontal lobe from functioning, and before you know it, you're blabbering to your pious, protective grandmother that you're not a virgin.

"Gina?" My name is more a warning.

"I-I…" There's nothing for me to say. She either accepts it or tosses me out.

She stands and paces. She hasn't removed the scarf that covers her head, and I half expect her to walk out the door and come in again pretending the last five minutes never happened.

"What do you remember about Chris Rinaldi?" She stands above me.

"He and his family lived three houses down. He was the youngest until Carina came along. He and I were ten when she was born. He went to the Catholic school, like most kids on the block. He left for college after Carina died. We had graduated high school. I moved in with you soon after. My mother had given up on me by then, hadn't she?"

Nonna waves her hand. "I'm not going to deal with your worthless mother right now."

A lump of lead forms in my stomach. I've never heard Nonna say a bad word about her daughter, or how she abandoned me.

"It's the Rinaldi girl, the baby. Can you remember?" Her eyes get sad, and I fight through the autistic haze to grasp at the events.

Recalling memories without emotions is like reciting the multiplication table. I can do it, but I've got to turn on that part of my brain.

His sister was much younger than he was. I played with her. I liked her because she played games when kids my age wouldn't play with me.

She was in the kiddy pool.

I was in the kiddy pool.

"Nonna." I can't get a breath. I try to breathe in, but no air comes. My body shakes. I relive that moment when I splashed water at Carina and tickled her. She liked being tickled.

She dunked under. And came up. And dunked under again.

"Nonna?" I shiver despite the heavy August night.

She rushes to my side. "Nothing came out of the investigation. It rained, and there was chaos."

"It did rain. We got out of the pool. All of us. Carina, too." I grab my head. It hurts. It pounds.

"It wasn't your fault, no matter what." She hugs me, and her rose-scented perfume gags me instead of bringing its usual comfort.

I pull away. "What do you mean, 'no matter what'?"

"Even if you had something to do with it, how could you have known?"

"I wasn't an idiot before the medication. I knew right from wrong. I knew not to kill little girls." It's my turn to stalk around the tiny living room. "This is why Mother left. She thought I drowned Carina

Rinaldi. She couldn't stand the shame. It was bad enough having the daughter who could never have friends, never amount to anything. But to have a daughter who was an accidental murderer — that was the straw for her, wasn't it?" I learned my steely glare from the best, so Nonna recognizes it when she sees it.

She nods. "I tried to talk to her, but..." She pulls out her rosary. "It's my fault as much as hers. If I had raised her better, she wouldn't have married that no-good man who left when you were a baby, and she would have lived up to her responsibilities."

"If she hadn't married my no-good father, my no-good mother never would've had me. Would that have been for the best?"

"That's not what I meant, Gina."

I hold up my hand. I run up the stairs and bang my door shut. The framed photos of old New York rattle against the wall.

The rumpled sheets on my bed and the dark stain bring the entire evening back to me.

I accept that if you want to feel emotions, you have to take the bad with the good.

But the horrendous with the amazing — that's too much burden.

Give me a derivative pricing equation any day of the week over a disappointed grandmother, an elated lover, and a haunting memory.

CHRIS

Genloran's stock price bounces around a bit, but for the most part holds steady. The word from my expert is that any day now they'll release the results of their phase two trial, which until this point only I have known about. He assured me the FDA has already approved phase three, which is under way, and then the miracle pill will hit the market. It will be in the hands of listless people everywhere.

Bob Breckner stops in my doorway.

"Chris, I gotta hand it to you. That last report on the medical device company did the trick. Looks like our traders are outselling the boys at Goldman. Where you get your information I don't know, but we're killing today."

"Thanks, Bob." The rush of adrenaline through my blood hits my brain, and I know the next promotion will be mine. "I think you'll be happy once Genloran announces, too."

He pats the doorjamb. "No doubt I will. And I think you'll be happy come bonus time." He shoots his finger gun and walks away.

"Yes." I slam my fist on the table. How can everything be turning out so magically for me?

My career is taking off just months after I started. I've got a girl who is so low maintenance she makes me look needy. And I can bury my past. The clock shows four-thirty. I won't have to work late, and Gina will arrive any minute. I'll take her to a nice dinner and back to my place, where we won't have to worry about her grandmother coming home. Yesterday wasn't how I would have wanted her first time to be, but it wasn't a complete disaster. These things are always tricky, and she seemed thrilled afterward. Her emotions are infectious because they are so new.

My intercom buzzes.

"Chris, you have a delivery here, and the man says he has to give it to you personally."

"I'm not expecting anything."

"Yes…well."

"Fine, fine. Send him back."

I search Yelp for the perfect romantic place to take Gina. Something classy, but not so much that she feels uncomfortable. Something where she can order her ginger ale.

"You forgot your bag at the house." Marco stomps into my office and dumps my bag on the floor.

"Thanks." I get up and come around to greet him, but his expression lets me know that he's in no mood for a brotherly hug.

"That was a nice performance you put on for Pop's birthday." He wanders around the room and inspects my diplomas.

"I didn't plan it." My older brother can't kick the crap out of me anymore, but that doesn't stop the neurons from firing and bringing back all the ass kickings he gave me when his face got that deadly serious look.

"Nope, you probably didn't. But I don't think screwing around with Gina Giancarlo was an accident."

"It sort of was." I scratch my head.

"I don't buy that. You have your pick of these city girls." He turns to survey Cubeville. "So what gives?"

He plops uninvited into the visitor chair Gina picked out.

"Don't you have to make more deliveries?" I sit behind my desk and tap a pen against my keyboard.

"Done for the day, and the truck's parked in a loading zone. I got time." He laces his fingers behind his head and leans back.

"All these years, I've tortured myself. I was so sure I was the one who let Carina drown. You know how Pop made sure we took that responsibility to heart." I take a deep breath and avoid looking at Marco's hard stare. "I ran. I shouldn't have. I should have trusted in our family. I didn't even know there was an investigation."

"Yeah, if you had done the stand-up thing and been here, you would have." He puts his hands on his knees and rises. "They didn't prove anything, though. Gina might have been playing rough with Carina, but once the thunder and lightning started...madness. You would think it had never rained in Kew Gardens before. Gina didn't testify. They said she was incompetent." He leans forward. "Still, Momma and the others associate Gina with that day. And you mean to tell me you can't find no other place to put your dick besides her?"

"Don't you dare talk about her that way. It isn't what you think. And until yesterday, my dick was nowhere near her." Ass kicking or no ass kicking, I come right up to his face, even a few inches above him now.

"I don't even get why you want to be with a girl like that." Marco's sneer sends a wave of rage right through the top of my head.

"Like what? Brilliant at math? A girl with an innate eye for design who's headed to college for a real career? A girl who discovers each new emotion and cherishes it? A girl who is kind and giving? A girl who doesn't play head games because she doesn't know how? A girl who doesn't demand every second of my time or get jealous? A girl who just recently learned to love and showed me how to return love?"

Surprise crosses Marco's face as he steps back to avoid my spit.

His expression is mirrored in the faces of the people packing up to leave for the day. Cubeville has stopped all work to stare into my office.

I close my mouth and swallow. I'm the most

surprised out of any of them.

"Well, I guess my work here is done." Marco regains the badass persona he adopts when he comes into the city. It's his way of coping with not having made it outside Queens except in his delivery truck.

"I'll come by the house next week and make amends." I sink into my desk chair.

"Bring some wine for Momma. It's going to take more than your charm and good looks to get out of this one." He pauses in the doorway. "And if you're serious about Gina, you'd better make it a case of wine."

The show is over, and everyone scurries to get the elevators down. I check my phone. Gina hasn't texted, but I'm sure she's on her way.

I write and rewrite the same paragraph of my next analysis, but Gina still doesn't call. I text her to find out where she is.

No answer.

I shut down my computer and go down to wait for her in the lobby.

I pace for another ten minutes. She's never late. Her mind has a way of keeping time so she arrives exactly on the dot.

She doesn't answer my calls or texts, so I walk toward the coffee shop. Maybe I'll meet her coming the other way.

Perks Plus is shutting down for the day. I spot Sarah.

"Hey, did Gina leave?"

She's pulling down the metal gate. "She left early today. She had to meet with someone at the center."

"We had plans..."

Sarah shrugs. Something in her manner tells me she knows more than she's saying.

"What?"

"It's not my place to say." She snaps the lock in place and walks away.

The Autism Center isn't far, and I hail a cab. A sinking feeling in my stomach tells me that maybe last night was a terrible idea.

It's not the first time I've let my cock get me into trouble. It's just the first time I've ever cared.

I pay the cab and read the directory. The Autism Center for Adults is on the third floor. I've got to talk to Gina, let her know I'm sorry for taking her so roughly. I'll make it up to her in any way she wants. I'll take a vow of chastity. Okay, maybe not that far.

The doors open and people mill about. There seems to be a group headed down the hall.

"Can I help you?" the woman behind the desk asks.

"I'm looking for someone. Gina Giancarlo. She's a friend and she didn't show up for our date, and I'm worried. Someone at her job said she'd come here."

"I'm sorry, sir. I can't confirm or deny that your friend is a client here. Or give out any information about our clients."

"I understand. But I think she's upset, and I'm worried. I don't want anything to happen to Gina." Fear like I haven't felt in years grips my lungs.

"Are you Chris?" A tall woman dressed in professional black slacks and a cheap version of a designer blouse approaches me.

"Yes. You know Gina?"

"I can't confirm or deny that."

"Come on. Can't someone see that I'm worried about her?"

She beckons me to a sitting area with worn, mismatched upholstered furniture. I briefly think about what Gina must say about it.

"I'm Jennifer Berger and I'm one of the social workers here. I can't talk to you about our clients, but I can educate you about autism."

I want to leap up and scream that I don't want to learn about autism, but she's at least being friendly to me.

"There are lots of different ways autism can manifest itself. Some people never develop verbal skills, while others become brilliant innovators in their fields. The autistic mind works differently — some see in pictures and some in numbers, and some have both. But whichever way it does, it gives the person with autism a different perspective than the rest of us. It can come at a price. They don't experience emotions the same way."

"I know all this just from being with Gina."

"But maybe you don't know that things you and I take for granted can be overwhelming. They need time to adjust to changes in relationships, changes in routines—any small change can trigger a panic reaction and some regression."

"But she was doing so well. She was acting normal."

"I can't comment on that. But autism doesn't go away, no matter how much progress a person makes. It's like having brown hair. You can dye it blonde, but underneath you're still a brunette."

"And I thought I was an expert at picking out the naturals."

"Huh?"

"Never mind. Thanks, Jennifer." I stand and shake her hand.

"You're welcome." She takes a long look at me. "I can't comment on specific clients, but sometimes they tell me that *praying* helps."

"Now I'm confused."

"Sometimes clients tell me they are *going to church* to pray." She jerks her head toward the window.

A Catholic church across the street is framed in the window.

"Oh. I can see how that might be helpful. Thanks again."

Jennifer sent her message loud and clear. Not

just where I can find Gina. But Gina needs time. We need to go slow. I can do that. I could back up and start again with her.

Maybe I haven't ever gone slowly with any other woman, and maybe I've never tried to have a relationship before. But there is no reason I can't do it now.

Slow, no big changes.

Other than the fact that our families hate each other, Gina has autism, and I have no experience in romantic relationships, what could go wrong?

Chapter 13

GINA

The priest isn't hearing confessions now. There's a velvet rope blocking access to the box.

When I was little, that box freaked me out. The dark closet reminded me of the timeout corner in school.

Now, I would welcome its inhospitable embrace. I need some formal way to cope with my thoughts.

I almost didn't take my medication this morning. Automatically, I took the pill bottle from the cabinet in the bathroom, shook out one chalky white tablet, and held it in my hand.

Powder from the pill spilled across my palm. If I didn't take it, I could go back. Go back to not feeling anything, not thinking about anything other than numbers and color swatches and perfectly matching the Crate and Barrel display in Nonna's living room.

I shoved it to the back of my throat and gulped some water.

Even though I took my pill this morning, I went through the workday without feeling much. The brain has a way of shutting down when it's overwhelmed. I guess losing my virginity, finding out I might have drowned a little girl, and discovering the reason my mother abandoned me was enough to crash the system.

Sarah pestered me all day, asking what was wrong. I think she was worried that I had regressed to my old self, since I didn't smile or talk much.

I couldn't bring myself to tell her everything. Only that I had sex with Chris, and Nonna was upset. I hinted that our families hate each other for things in the past. She was ready to kick Chris's ass, but I assured her he had done nothing wrong.

A light from the back flashes. Someone has entered the church. I'm alone in the pew, and except for the caretaker who has been replenishing the candles in the side chapel, I'm the only person here.

Footsteps approach. Someone on leather-soled shoes takes purposeful strides and stops in the aisle next to me.

I know before I look up. His scent and his energy are intimately familiar to me. I know his emotional state more than I know my own.

I slide over and he sits next to me. The heat from his leg radiates to mine. I want to lean my head against his shoulder, have him trail his fingers through my hair and tell me it's going to be okay.

"How'd you find me?"

"Your social worker, Jennifer, gave me a hint."

"She broke about five HIPAA laws and her code of ethics."

"Maybe she thought it was important."

The church is dark, except for a few lights high above and the colored patterns of the stained-glass windows. Nonna wouldn't like them because they are abstract designs instead of scenes depicting some saint performing a miracle.

"I've sinned." I still can't bring myself to look at him. One glance at his green eyes and square jaw and I couldn't trust my body or my heart.

"I guess it is a sin." He fidgets with his hands, careful not to reach out to me. "But plenty of people do it before they are married. And I think confession can clear it up."

"No. Not that. I don't regret sex. Not really." He must know, and has never said anything. The whole neighborhood knew. My own mother wanted nothing to do with me. "Why me? Chris, why did you pick me? I know you can date normal women."

"Gina, I have no idea. I wish I had some wonderfully romantic thing to say. The truth is that I asked you out to make a good impression on my bosses at that party, and...I got hooked on your honesty, your energy, the way you shoot from the hip." He leans over and drops his voice. "And your hips." He chuckles.

I can't keep the smile down, but it's not the big smile that opens my eyes. It's a small smile that makes tears come. "That is romantic. In a way." I find the courage to look at him. "Do you know?

About what happened with Carina?"

He dips his head. "Does anyone know?"

"Jennifer said the papers are public record. I can go read them."

"Why, Gina? Why would you do that?" He grasps my hands and nearly crushes them.

"Shouldn't I know the truth?" Tears are freely flowing down my face. "How can you bear to be with me? I probably killed your sister." My voice rises and stops the caretaker in his tracks as he shuffles to the rectory door.

"I had to bear being with myself all these years. I might be the one responsible. I left her alone in the pool right before it rained. I went to get a towel. The rain started. People were running."

"You left her in the pool with me." A strangled cry erupts from my throat and sobs shudder my body.

Chris gulps and I look up. His face is contorted and blotchy. Tears nearly squirt out of his eyes, and we grip each other.

"We're all sinners, Gina." He gasps into my hair.

GINA

Jennifer is taking way too long to meet me in her office. I don't even want to see her today, but something is going on with the study and she insisted. I can't tolerate sitting in her worn chair anymore.

I stand, face the window, and shove my hands into my pockets. I feel a chain and pull out a saint's medal Nonna has stuck in there. I grip it so tightly that it cuts into my palm. I thrust it back in my pocket. I doubt any saint will be watching over me today.

"Hi, Gina." Jennifer enters the room.

"You're late. I need to meet Chris in an hour. We're going to look up the records." I plop back into the chair and glare.

"I think that's a brave thing you're doing. I'm here if you want to call me later."

"Why should I want to call you?" Jennifer thinks I need her, but I don't. I don't need Nonna protecting me, or Jennifer telling me what to do.

"Are you angry at me for asking you to come in this morning?"

"Yeah, I'm busy. Chris is taking time off work to do this with me." I pick at the edge of the fraying seat.

"Besides having something else to do, what is making you angry about being here?"

"I get that I'm part of the study, so study me. They've measured everything from my IQ to my blood, and even asked about my bowel movements. What else do they want?"

Jennifer doesn't say anything, simply wears a neutral expression. How the heck am I supposed to figure out what's going on with her?

"Isn't that all I am to them? A test subject? Do they even care about what happens when you mess with people's emotions? Do you, Jennifer? Does this place?"

"Are you questioning whether I care about you?" Jennifer's expression doesn't alter.

"What's the point in coming here? I'm not really autistic anymore."

She raises her eyebrow, and I can't stand to look at her face. I bound up and turn to look out the window.

"If you want to discuss your treatment here, we can. If you're continuing in the study, you'll have to keep seeing me. After that, well, we can make other plans."

I've always had a social worker. I've always seen therapists. Could I really do away with them?

"I'm scared." The words croak out of me.

"Anyone would be. What you're doing by looking up the records of Carina's death, it opens up old wounds. There isn't a person, autistic or not, who wouldn't be scared."

"It's not that. It's not being autistic. I've always been autistic. What happens when I stop?"

"Will you stop?"

"Don't you think I have?" I can't face her. I don't want to read her answer on her face.

"The drug company sure thinks so. They wanted

you to sign these forms allowing them to publish their initial findings in a journal."

I hear her shuffle some papers, but I can't turn around.

"What am I if I'm not autistic?"

"Gina, turn around." Jennifer's voice has become weary.

I shuffle back to the seat.

"I have no idea what to tell you about this. It's new and unexpected. I don't even think the pharmaceutical company expected results like this. That's why they're rushing things along. But you can't base your identity on a pharmaceutical company, a medication, or even a diagnosis. You need to define yourself in your own terms." She chuckles. "And if there's anyone who has their own terms, it's you."

"Am I doing the right thing? Looking into the past?"

She shrugs. "I have no idea what I would do in your position. But it does seem that if you and Chris want any future together, you've got to straighten out the past."

"Sorry I was such a bitch before." I slide the papers toward me and grab a pen from her desk.

"It's my pleasure to see you being a bitch." She touches my arm. "I'm reveling in the full range of your expressions."

"At least someone is."

CHRIS

"We don't have to go through with this." I squeeze Gina's hand as we wait at the clerk's desk.

The records department of the Queens County coroner's office does nothing to ease the anxiety people feel entering this place — the harsh fluorescent lighting, the long linoleum hallway, the walls adorned with nothing but informational posters explaining overtime laws, and the posed school pictures of the clerk's three children Scotch-taped to the side.

"Yes, I do. I can't stand not remembering." Gina bounces on the balls of her feet. She wears a pair of jeans that hug her hips, and her shirt plunges low. It's wrong that even now I'm thinking about getting with her.

For the past two days we haven't gone down that path. Not that there was much opportunity. Her grandmother has kept her on a tight leash, and she's been too wrapped up in her investigation to think about sex.

"I gotta hand it to you. I would have had no idea how to find these records." I watch the clerk coming toward us with a stack of papers.

"It wasn't so hard. I just called the office and put in a request. They're charging me a copy fee because I want to be able to read it at home." She takes her eyes off the approaching office worker and scans the room. "I can't imagine spending another minute longer in here."

"That's twenty-four ninety-five." He slaps the papers on the counter.

"Here, let me." I wave away Gina's wallet, reach into my pocket, and hand the guy a ten and a twenty.

"We don't make change. I need the exact amount or a money order from a US bank."

"They didn't say that on the phone." Gina's voice rises.

"Keep it." I pick up the papers and grab Gina's elbow.

"I can't keep it." The guy wears the cheapest white shirt I've ever seen. You can see through it to his undershirt, which has a stain on the front. "Giving me extra money is bribing a government official."

"Donate it to the Christmas party fund," I call over my shoulder, and hustle Gina out.

The sun beats down on us. The end of August is a bitch in the city, even in Queens.

"You want me to take you home?" I direct Gina to the corner, where I think I can find a cab.

She shakes her head. "Nonna will be there. I don't know where to go."

"You wanna go to a coffee shop?"

"No." She shrinks against me. At five foot two, she's not tall, but she seems even smaller.

"Okay, we're going to my place." I spot a livery cab and yank the door open. I even agree to the outrageous fare he wants to charge to go back into Manhattan.

Gina snuggles into my side. "Maybe it was a mistake. Maybe you just wasted thirty dollars."

"Listen, just because we have this doesn't mean we need to read it now. We can keep it. When you feel ready, then read it." Her hair springs back into place after I gently tug a curl.

"You're right. What does it even matter now?" Her voice is not convincing. It matters. It matters because it's our past. Our future can't arrive until we know how we started.

She's silent all the way into the city. We reach my building and Jack the doorman opens the door.

"Home in the middle of the day?" He raises his eyebrows and holds the front door open for Gina, giving her ass a once-over.

"Don't I tip you enough at Christmas?" I grumble as I follow her inside.

She stops in the center of the lobby and cranes her neck around. "Chris, are you rich?"

I've gotten used to the marble and mirrored walls. An apartment on the Upper East Side doesn't come cheap, and despite the mouthy doorman, I've always been proud of it. But through Gina's working-class eyes, I'm a little humbled.

"No. I guess I wanted something different than

where I grew up."

She breaks her gaze from the potted palms and joins me at the elevator.

"It's not so impressive once you're inside." I wrap my arm around her waist and kiss the top of her head. I've never brought a woman to my place. And only a few of my brothers have been here. Rob's been over, but no one else.

I have this upscale apartment, and I've never shown it off to anyone. And now that I have the chance to brag, I feel silly. I exit the elevator and Gina follows down the hall. The high-end address seems frivolous now. Tucked under my arm might be the answer to questions I've beaten myself up with over the past six years.

"You're right, it is small." Gina walks in and surveys my junior one-bedroom.

The bed is in a different room, which means it's a one-bedroom and not a studio, but there's no room to walk completely around the bed.

"From anyone else that would sound like an insult. From you, the truth." I indicate for her to sit on the leather couch that hardly anyone has sat on. I grab a ginger ale and a beer from the fridge.

"You got me ginger ale." She takes a long swallow.

"I've been waiting for you to visit me." I sit next to her. The stack of copies from the coroner's office sits on the stone-topped coffee table. "You sure about this?"

"Are you?" Her eyes grow wider, and although she looks like the most innocent person ever, I know she's tougher than her kitten eyes show.

"We might as well."

One by one we trade pages of the proceedings. The first few pages are mostly dull, and cover formalities.

Gina gasps, takes a small section, and puts it to the side.

"What?"

"The pathologist's report. The autopsy." She covers part of her face with the papers.

"Yeah, let's skip those." The last thing I need is to hear the details of my sister's body cut to pieces.

But the coroner's testimony is there. Carina died by drowning, but there was a bruise on the back of her head. Whether she got the bruise before falling into the pool, or in the pool, he couldn't tell. Was she unconscious when she entered the water, or got the bruise right after she drowned in the confusion of kids running when the thunder started, he couldn't say.

I take another swig of beer and divorce my mind from my heart. If Gina can withstand going through these papers, then I can too.

"Here it is." She sits up and leans over to show me. "Here's the part where my grandmother testifies. She said that I was incompetent. The DA admitted a report from my school and some psychologist. Nonna had filed for conservatorship then." She looks at me, and her green eyes shimmer with tears. "They didn't even want to hear what I had to say. I remember. I remember playing with Carina. I remember the storm. She got out of the pool. I even helped her out. I swear to you, Chris. She was out of the pool when the storm started."

"I believe you. Why wouldn't they listen to you back then?" I bring a sheet closer to my face to read the affidavit that Gina was incompetent to be a witness. "She was out of the pool when the storm hit." I hear myself say the words as if someone else is speaking them. Because it can't be true. It isn't the story I told myself all these years.

Does that lessen my guilt? Us older kids were all responsible for Carina, and the lifeguard told me the pool was clear. I assumed that she headed the three blocks back to our house. She knew the way. "Carina wasn't left in the pool by anyone."

"I know that. I've always known that."

"I know, I believe you." I shush her and pat her arm. She jerks away.

"But it doesn't matter what you believe. Nonna must have thought it was my fault. She tried to protect me, but I didn't need protection then. And I don't need protection now."

I reflect on what I've read. We'll never know how or why Carina died. The truth is that the

135

moment I stepped away was the moment the sky opened up. Could I have found her before she drowned? There was such chaos. The finding was accidental death. The coroner's best guess was that she exited the pool and fell back in when everyone went screaming.

"You don't need protection," I agree. "I've never met anyone with a clearer direction, or better able to care for herself."

"I think I'll go to court." Gina straightens the papers and pushes them away. "I don't need a conservator."

"No, you don't. I'll help you fight it if you want." I mean the words, but they don't come out as strong as I want them to.

"I'm sorry. I've forgotten about how all this makes you feel." She reaches around my shoulders. She's too small for me to lean on, but the gesture is comforting.

"It's good to know that at least we'll never know." Her scent is warm, and there's a bit of cinnamon still stuck to her pants from work.

"Thanks for taking the afternoon off to do this with me. I know you're busy at work."

"There's nothing I wouldn't do for you." The words are out of my mouth before I think them.

"I know." She slants toward me for a kiss.

When I claim her mouth with mine, I'm not just kissing her, I'm making a promise. The past is behind us, and we'll stand together for whatever the future brings.

She presses her chest against me, and her breasts push up higher, almost spilling out of her shirt.

"Gina, I can go slow," I plead.

"Yes, like last time, only better." She tugs at my shirt to lift it over my head. "Oh." She trails her hands down my chest and runs a finger under the waistband of my pants.

I don't even try to stifle the groan. I can't play it cool with Gina. She brings me to my knees, literally. So I go with it and kneel in front of her, help her wriggle out of her pants.

Lacy black panties cover her mound.

"Mmmm." I dip a finger underneath, and she's already wet.

"Sarah said I needed real lingerie." Her words come out in gasps because I'm working her clit.

She arches her back, offering more access. I nearly rip the "real lingerie" off her.

"Can I taste you?" I look up into her face, which is transformed by passion. She's lost that critical thinking expression. She's all emotion now.

She bites her lower lip and nods.

She flinches as I get close. I pause, but she raises her hips to meet my mouth.

I dart my tongue out and brush it against the soft flesh.

"Oh." She eases back into the couch and lets her

legs fall apart. I tease her, licking along the inside of her thigh and then gently sucking on her clit. She tastes salty and smells of that lemony soap she uses.

Her breaths increase and she cries out a yelp and pushes against me. I stop, blow some cool air across her moist curls, and lay her flat on the couch.

"I didn't finish." Her eyes widen.

"You will." I unbutton her blouse and unhook her bra before she even responds. I do have my talents.

She giggles as she helps me off with my pants.

"You have to stop laughing when I get naked," I grumble, and scoop her up and carry her into the tiny bedroom. I playfully plop her on the bed.

She giggles more, and I don't really mind because it makes her tits move in the most enticing way. I climb over her and take her tit in my mouth and roll her nipple around with my tongue.

She reaches down and grabs my cock. Her small hands tease me, and all I want is more friction.

"Can I taste you?"

"Oh God, yes." I roll off her and she climbs between my legs.

Her hair falls over and I can't see the lower half of my body, but her full lips envelop me, and her teeth scrape against my skin. I'm on freaking fire, and it's all I can do to keep from coming in her mouth. Her hands explore every inch of my body she can reach from down there. Her touch is gentle and hot.

"Gina." Her name is a prayer more serious than anything I've ever said in church. Because right now I'd do anything for her.

She pops off. "You didn't finish yet either." Her mischievous grin says it all.

"I've got a condom in here." I open the side drawer. "It's ribbed."

"Oooh." She lies next to me and watches in fascination as I roll it over my erection.

"I'll be slow." I don't want to hurt her again, savoring each blissful second.

I ease into her, and her channel wraps around my cock. I watch her face for any sign she might be uncomfortable, but her closed eyes flutter open, and she meets my gaze and smiles.

I move slowly and her body rocks with mine. The heat coming off her is blazing, and I'm consumed.

I start to lose rational thought, but I take one hand and use my thumb to finish the job that my tongue started.

She calls my name, bucks her hips, and thrashes her head from side to side. The muscles inside of her grip me, and I follow.

"Gina, I love you." I pump one last time into her and everything shatters—the walls I've built around myself for the past six years, the lies I tell myself about money making me happy, and the past secrets

Gina and I shared.

I fall to her side, panting. Her chest glistens with beads of sweat. The reality of my words hit me. I don't expect anything in return. And part of me is going to be okay no matter what happens with Gina.

She twirls a finger through my chest hair and her thoughtful expression returns.

"Christopher Rinaldi, I think I love you, too."

Chapter 14

GINA

It's no problem finding the classrooms. Each floor of the building where the design classes are taught is laid out with even numbers on one side, odd on the other. I count by prime numbers and regulate my breathing.

I am a fraud.

The other students take their seats at desks around the room. A few nod and say hello to me. I smile and return the greeting.

But they don't know that I am faking it. I have to think through each motion, remind myself to smile. Have the pills failed me today?

The professor comes in. He explains the syllabus and the class structure. I listen and take notes. I look just like the other students, but inside I'm autistic.

Earlier, Nonna offered to pack me a lunch, but I declined. I'm going to be too nervous to eat anyway. Nonna's face held all the fear I had been feeling, but I couldn't let on to her. She isn't strong enough to cope with my anxiety. She's spent the last six years protecting me from any kind of stress, anything that might set me off.

And now, even though I have only two classes a day, I don't think my heart will survive.

When I was eight, my mom dressed me in a princess costume for Halloween. I hated it. It itched like crazy and the skirts made an awful swishy noise when I walked. I spent the entire night on the edge of tears and trembling as my mom dragged me to each neighbor's house.

My back threatens to itch just as much now, as the professor brings up slides on the screen.

I'm no more a college student than I was a princess.

Gradually, I begin to lose myself in his lecture. He talks about the importance of dominance and focal points. And I'm interested. These ideas had come to me, but I could never put names to them. I like the way he categorizes the concepts, and the images on the smart board immediately spark ideas.

By the end of class, my breathing has slowed. The sweat on my back has dried. Maybe I can pull this off.

"I'm Zack. This is Franny. Your first day of classes, too?"

One...two...three...

"Yes, I'm Gina." I extend my hand and Zack gives it a pump. Franny smiles, and I pray my smile is as warm as hers.

"We work together at Sotheby's. Well, at least we used to. Threw it all away to be full-time students." Franny laughs and starts toward the door. She dips her head to indicate I should follow.

"I work at a coffee shop on Wall Street. Dropped my hours to accommodate the class schedule. But I can't afford to not work."

"We can't either. But we're pretending that sharing a closet of an apartment and eating rice and beans is normal," Zack says.

I laugh, and the exhale of air lessens the jangle of my nerves.

We discover that we all have the same class in another twenty minutes, and take seats in the student union coffee shop to wait.

Zack and Franny are friends, not dating.

"It would be easier if we could share a bed. Then there'd be room to turn around in the apartment." Zack takes a sip of his coffee.

"I live with my grandmother." The excuses of why I live with my grandmother run through my head. I can't tell them my mother abandoned me. I can't lie like Chris did and say I'm the one taking care of her.

"That's sweet. I bet it's nice to have home-cooked meals." Franny flips though the course list.

"Yeah. She's a little old-fashioned. Doesn't like my boyfriend. But at least I can afford tuition this way."

"Serious boyfriend?" Franny's eyebrows wiggle.

I chuckle. "Serious enough."

I have successfully fooled these two nice students. They have no idea that they're talking to a freak who has to remember how to say hello.

I make it through the next lecture and say good-bye to my new friends. If you can call people you have just conned friends.

I might have been prepared for the classes, for having to navigate a new place. But nothing prepared me for having to fool people. This is the first time I'm meeting people who don't already know all about me. I'm not sure if I'm angry at myself for not telling them about me, or if I'm angry with the way the world is set up so that I feel I need to warn people about my autism.

It's not far to the coffee shop, and I have plenty of time to get there for my afternoon shift. But I hustle anyway, my book bag slapping hard against my hip. I need the discomfort to keep me in the present.

I nearly break the door off the hinges as I enter Perks Plus.

"Whoa, there." Sarah's eyes go wide. "You okay?"

"Fine." I hear a tremble in my voice, and I will not cry.

I storm into the backroom, drop my bag, and tear my apron off the hook.

"You have to pay for the ones you rip." Becky leans against the doorframe.

"Fine," I mutter. I just need a few minutes before I start work.

"So today was your first day of school. Did you make friends? Give the teacher an apple?" she sneers.

"Becky, you hate me. I get it. I don't care for you much either. It doesn't matter to me one bit why you dislike me. But you've got to lay off. You must have a teaspoon of decency in you."

"You think you deserve special treatment just because you're autistic. You got this job through that nuthouse you go to. They hand out jobs to you people, while the rest of us have to apply and get rejected to make room for the special needs cases. Well, I don't think so." Her eyes bug out, and her face turns almost purple.

"You hate me because I'm different and because I've taken advantage of some extra help." I nod. "I get it. But I still don't care."

I edge past her and join Sarah at the counter.

"Were you two arguing back there? I thought I heard something," she mumbles to me as she makes change for a customer.

"No biggie." I rearrange the pastries and remove an empty platter. "Becky doesn't seem to want to work with a special needs person," I say as she emerges from the back with her bag slung over her shoulder.

"Becky?" Sarah's voice is a warning.

"I just think it's unfair."

I stand up from the display case. "You know what's unfair? Trying to fit into what everyone expects you to fit into. The narrow rules that I have to follow. The fact that my mother gave up on me, and my grandmother has never trusted me." My face is wet. Tears splatter onto my apron front, and I stride to Becky. My voice finds a steady cadence. "You don't know how fair you've had it. And don't ever talk to me that way again."

I take purposeful steps to the bathroom. I lock the door and wash my face. Becky is an asshole, but not the last asshole I'll have to deal with in my life.

The old me never had the strength, or even the awareness, to deal with the Beckys. This is one more hurdle to having deep emotions. I end up caring about what other people think. Crap.

It was easier without the awareness. I could let Becky sneer at me, and oh well, life went on. Now, I have to stand up for myself. And with entering school, and eventually a career, I suspect there will be tons more of these times ahead.

I take one more deep breath and rejoin Sarah.

"I'm not sure I can fire her for that. But I'll try." She pats my back.

"Don't bother. It's good practice for me." I wipe down the milk steamer.

"So, tell me everything about your first classes."

"It wasn't a disaster." I find myself smiling and relaxing. True friends can do that for you.

CHRIS

I hoof it over to the coffee shop. Gina texted me when classes were done. It's hard to tell from a text, especially one of Gina's texts, but she didn't sound happy.

I've got an afternoon meeting with Breckner and some others on where our pharma investments are going, so I can't be long. But I have to see her.

Last night we spent a good twenty minutes on the phone just saying, "I love you." I'm whipped. Sad that the stud I once was has been reduced to jogging over in the middle of the day to see a girl and talk about her schoolwork. Last time I cut out of work for a girl, it was to meet at the Hilton for a nooner.

Gina and Sarah are head to head in deep discussion. There aren't many customers, and they don't notice me when I enter.

Gina explains something while Sarah listens. Her mouth forms words I can't hear, but her face is alight with energy. I love it when she is like this. When something interests her, she is all consumed. Her concentration in complete. Not many people can throw themselves into anything as deeply as she can.

As I approach, they turn. Gina's face splits into a smile, but there is redness about her eyes.

"Hello, Christopher Rinaldi. A double-shot

mochaccino?" Her hand on her hip, she cocks her head and bats her eyes.

"Nah, just a wet, sloppy kiss, please."

She leans over the counter. The kiss doesn't last as long as I would like, but her boss is right there, and I can't complete the actions my brain is sending to my hands.

"Take a break, Gina." Sarah winks, and we sit at a table in the back.

"So, how did it go?" I hold her small hand in mine.

"Okay, I guess. The classes were interesting, and I met two other students who seemed friendly."

"But...?"

She shrugs. "I was so nervous. I felt myself slipping backwards."

"Backwards?"

"Into the old me. The one who couldn't remember to smile when I met someone new. Or even how to smile. I'm a freak." I'm about to argue with her when she shifts and takes her vibrating phone out of her pocket. Someone has texted her.

"Who is it?" I ask.

As she reads the message, a small grin forms at the corners of her mouth. Her mouth is accented with a red lipstick that I want to lick off.

"These two students I met today. Zack and Franny. They invited me out for drinks." She looks up, and her green eyes swim with joy. "They said to bring along my boyfriend."

"That's me." I stroke her arm, and the tiny shiver lets me know she likes that term as much as I do. "You must have done a better job than you thought. Zack and Franny aren't texting you because they thought you were a freak."

"I know, it's just… I had to really think about what to say and do. It was like before the pills—" She clamps a hand over her mouth.

"What?"

"Nothing. I'm not supposed to say. I-I…" She takes a deep breath. "You might as well know. I'm taking an experimental drug. It's what's been responsible for the change in me."

"A drug experiment?" Part of my brain screams for me to not ask. *Don't go there, Chris.*

"I forget what they call it. But it's a phase three trial. Not sure what that means. Are you okay?" She runs her hand across my back. It would normally calm me, but nothing is going to stop this gnawing in the back of my brain unless we change the subject.

"Gina, it doesn't matter what drug you're taking. You're you, and I love you." I kiss the palm of her hand. I need to end this conversation.

"Chris, will you really help me figure out how to end my conservatorship? It might send Nonna over the edge, but after today I'm convinced I need to be my own person."

"Sweetheart, whatever you want. I really need to

go. There's a meeting I can't be late for."

"So go. Can you meet for drinks tomorrow night with Franny and Zack?"

"You bet." I wave good-bye to Sarah and burst onto the sidewalk.

The temperature has cooled so I can break into a jog to get back to work.

I convince myself that Gina didn't tell me anything I shouldn't know. Besides, there are hundreds of drug trials going on all the time. There's nothing to connect what she said to Genloran.

And even if she is part of the study, that can't count as insider knowledge. I mean, she's my girlfriend, not part of my family. There's got to be some kind of girlfriend clause.

I can't let anything stop me now. Maybe one day I'll want to marry Gina, and I'll need the financial ability to do so. I need this gamble to pay out. No matter what.

Chapter 15

GINA

I've never been so bone-weary in my life.

I trudge down the hall to Jennifer's office. The anxiety and excitement from the first day of classes has given way to exhaustion. Standing on my feet for even the half a shift at the coffee shop was enough to leave my feet aching.

Her door is open, but I knock on the frame.

"Gina, it's so good to see you. Come in. I can't wait to hear all about it."

I plop into her overstuffed chair. I don't go to group anymore. I get private sessions with Jennifer. Which is better, since I don't have to deal with the other clients who don't seem to be progressing as rapidly. But it does mean I need to fill the entire hour with my own issues.

The only thing harder than dealing with emotions is talking about dealing with emotions.

"It's been a long day. But I think a good one." I rehash the day's events, ending with my confronting Becky. "I didn't tell Chris about that part." I chew my bottom lip.

"Gina, you don't have to share every detail with him all the time. When you're comfortable, you can tell him. Or not. I think it's something worth bragging about. You stood up for yourself in a way you've never been able to do before."

"I felt good and bad at the same time. Crap. I hate that part of feelings. That you can feel opposite ways simultaneously. Why can't they get a pill for that?"

"If they did, I'd be out of a job." Jennifer taps her pen on the desk. "And it sounds like you did a great job making friends."

"I didn't even approach them. They came up to me." I stare at the corner of her office where a cobweb has formed on the ceiling. "When do I have to tell them about me?"

"What about you?"

"Come on, Jennifer. I can't go around pretending to be normal. At some point Zack and Franny and all my professors will have to know."

"Why?"

"You're being difficult. Because sometime soon, I'm going to say or do something odd. I'm going to show that I'm not as clued in to the world of people and relationships. They think I'm just a regular girl, with a boyfriend, living with my grandmother to save money, and going to school."

"And what part of that is false?"

"Just the regular part."

"Gina, you never have to tell anyone anything. So what if you are a little quirky at times? There are worse things to be. And plenty of people who are Level One, like you, go on to have successful careers and never need to explain themselves at all. I'm sure Zack and Franny will grow to like your warmth and kindness, and forgive, if not enjoy, your quirkiness." She holds up a hand to stop me from interrupting her. "As for the regular part, who's to say what's regular? And plenty of people with autism go to college and graduate school and have hugely successful careers. This is something you could have done long before the medicine."

"I want to end my conservatorship. I want to have my own bank account and be a real adult." It comes out as more of a question than I wanted it to be.

Jennifer nods and taps the desk more. "You mentioned that last week." She sighs. "I think you'd be able to do that. If I were asked, I couldn't give a reason why you would be unable to be responsible. But it's all very new. You might want to wait a few months."

"Nonna has tried to protect me from the world. But I don't need protection. Chris said he'd help me."

"No, you don't need protection from the world." Jennifer gives a half-smile.

"But?" Here's the thing with being clued in to people's emotions and tones of speech: I can tell

153

when they're holding back. People have thoughts they don't want to share, but their emotions give them away.

My brain used to keep me from experiencing emotions fully. Now I realize that people's emotions keep their brains from functioning fully.

"I'm still concerned about Chris. No, let me finish. He hasn't done anything wrong. He's been respectful of you and seems completely genuine in his feelings for you. But he has a lot going on. He's dealing with trying to reconnect with his family at the same time he's formed a relationship with you, the one person who can keep the wedge between him and his family. He has issues, and I don't want you caught in the middle of them."

Even though my face gets hot and my insides twist, I know Jennifer is right.

"Yeah, he has issues. But it's not like I'm going to marry him. I have a chance to have a boyfriend, and it's fun and I don't want to mess that up."

"Fair enough." She sighs. "Our time is up, but stop by the nurse's office for your refill. And to complete the questionnaire for the study."

"Thanks." I don't stand immediately. "Really, I mean it. I'm thankful you take the extra time with me."

Jennifer's eyes become moist, and she sniffs. "I'm happy for you, Gina. And it's an honor to be along with you for this ride."

I stand and we hug. The last time I hugged Jennifer, it was just because it was part of a skill I was working on. But hugging is a great way to say something to someone you care about without words. It says, "I'm vulnerable with you and trust you. I'll let you get real close to me because we share things that mere friends don't."

Down the hall, the nurse dispenses medications and has a tiny office where she checks my blood pressure and temperature.

She has a calm, sweet face and pink scrubs.

"Here you go. Another month's worth." She hands me the plastic bottle with the safety lid. "And here's the questionnaire to fill out."

"It's the same questions every time." I take the pen and tick off the boxes indicating whether I've had side effects, what I have noticed in my moods, blah blah blah.

"Hi, Jerome," the nurse chirps. "Have a seat. I'll take your blood pressure."

Jerome sits opposite me in the cramped space. There's not more than a foot between our knees, and the nurse needs to maneuver around us to get her equipment.

"I took the medicine. I took the medicine." Jerome must be getting a placebo. He obviously hasn't made any progress.

I study him from under my hair that has fallen over my face as I bend over the paper. He squirms in his seat as the pressure cuff inflates. His eyes widen in near panic as the whoosh of air comes out.

I tense my fingers around the pen. I know those signs. The constriction of the pressure cuff, the alarming hiss of air. For someone with autism, those things can set off a full-blown meltdown. I can't remember having those meltdowns often. But I certainly have seen my fair share at the center.

The next question asks me about how many people I talk with during the day. And about my comfort level with conversations. I glance at Jerome again as he struggles to keep the thermometer under his tongue. The twist in my chest gets tighter.

How is it that I get to have these changes, and Jerome doesn't? It's not fair, and I can only hope that when the experiment is over, they give him the real drug. Because even though he's always bugged me by repeating himself, everyone deserves to experience the world the way I do now.

Even though I'd be condemning him to a life of conflicting and confusing emotions.

CHRIS

Breckner enters the conference room as I scoot in behind him. Senior analysts and a few other junior analysts are already seated around the table.

I slide into a chair and rest my hands on the table. My mind is focused now on the task at hand.

Gina and everything that goes along with her are safely tucked into a dark fold of my brain, and I will not access that information at all.

Breckner opens by going over the quarterly reports. He's happy, but it's never enough. If it were ever enough, I'd be out of a job. A few others chime in with recommendations about pharma and medical device companies. I'm so glad I didn't get assigned to the agribusiness team. Soybeans are dull, and the profits are slim. But medicine. People will sell their houses to stay alive with the latest medications.

"And Chris Rinaldi has some further recommendations. Chris?"

That's my cue. "Thanks, Bob." I launch into the recommendations I developed based on internal company reports from Genloran and intel gleaned from a guy I know who attended the big pharma convention. Those reports are never completely "internal." But I don't let on as to how I got the info.

"So Genloran is poised to make a splash. This wonder drug allows people to control their emotions, and it should address a range of disorders from schizophrenia to depression to autism." I choke on the last word. Yes, I read the reports, and knew that this drug was for autism, but I never made the connection. I never even knew Gina was taking medication, let alone the one I was betting my career on.

"Chris?"

Breckner tries to get my attention.

"Sorry, something stuck in my throat." I cough. "I'm confident that Genloran will be bought up by one of the bigger companies. One that has the production and marketing capabilities to get this drug into the hands of almost every psychiatric patient."

Appreciative murmurs rumble through the room. Breckner brings up some last-minute points and adjourns the meeting.

"Chris, a word," he says as people file out.

I sit back down at the table. He's at the head, and about ten feet of highly polished wood separate us.

"Your work on the medical device company paid off last quarter. And I see that all the extra time you spend with the traders seems to help them understand the recommendations, and that's increasing volume."

"Thanks. I enjoy that part."

He nods. "Your ass is on the line, you know that? It's a bold move, and all the glory will come your way, but also all the blame."

"Sure."

"I've been in this position for twenty years. At some point, my wife is going to demand I retire and spend half the year in Florida puttering around our beachfront house and taking the yacht out." He shakes his head. "I can't stand the idea. But I guess that's why I've worked so hard." He gazes out the window. "My yearly bonus is more than your entire salary. Did you know that?"

"I could have guessed." My stomach clenches. Part of me expects Breckner to fire me. The other part expects him to leap from the fifteenth floor to avoid spending every day with his wife in Boca Raton.

"Some kids take the long view. That if they perform just above average and wait it out, they'll move up." He returns his gaze to me. "And then there are those who want a fast track to the top and don't care if they cut a few corners."

"I was never good at going slow." I force some manly confidence into my voice.

"Neither was I. You're a smart one. Just watch those corners." He stands and pats my shoulder as he leaves the room.

The building across the street is reflected on the surface of the conference table. In each square sits another person working to get a share of the pile.

Breckner has a winter house and a yacht. But he shudders at the thought of living there with his wife.

Marco lives in a duplex in Queens. The closest he's come to Boca is the one trip to Disney with his kids. And I'm sure he thinks the sailboat he went on once with his work buddy is a yacht. And he manages to be happier.

Would I ever want to share a house of any size with Gina? Would her sometimes-odd behaviors get in the way at work parties? It's who she is, and I like her that way. But I can't ever see her fitting in with Mrs. Breckner at the spa.

It's too late now to turn back. I made my recommendations. I gave my reports based on the intel I had. I only hope that no one links me to the two experts who should have never spoken to me. Or that Gina takes a different medicine. Or maybe I want her to take the super drug. Maybe I want her to be less autistic.

Does that make me a bad person? Probably no worse than how I've thought of myself for the past six years.

GINA

Nonna and I wait in the hall outside the small courtroom. The papers are signed and stamped by a notary, and I lay them in my lap so my sweaty palms don't wrinkle them.

Nonna grips her sensible black purse and stares at the opposite wall, where a poster about DUIs hangs.

"It's going to be fine." I rest my hand on her arm.

She opens her mouth to speak but closes it again.

"You're scared for me. I'm scared, too. But I need to do this."

She turns to me. "What if the medicine stops working? What if you can't finish school?"

"Nonna, I'll be fine."

"Promise me that Christopher won't become your conservator. I couldn't stand that."

"He loves me, Nonna. Really. For who I am, autism and all. We'll never know what happened to Carina, but Chris doesn't blame me, and he doesn't deserve our blame."

"He was never any good. Out of all the Rinaldis, he was the most trouble. Always with the making noise and the graffiti on the walls."

I don't respond, because he *was* a terror as a kid. But he's managed to take all that energy and channel it into an MBA and a career. He needs to be a bit of a risk taker for his job.

"But he's also the only one to go to college." Nonna's words squeeze through her nearly clamped lips. "He makes a good living."

"Yes, he does." A tear escapes my eye, and I brush it away. "But I won't let anyone support me. I'm going to have my own career."

"Good."

"But, Nonna?"

"Hmmm?"

"Can I live with you a while longer?"

"I suppose you have to while you're in school." She huffs.

I bend over and kiss her cheeks. She smiles briefly. The doors open, and we're called inside.

I take her hand and walk into the courtroom. I

can remember holding her hand the same way six years ago. Only now I'm the one giving her comfort. Better than being able to have a regular conversation. Better than feeling proud, happy, and sad. Better than forming deep relationships. Being strong enough to support someone else — that's the best emotion.

CHRIS

Gina lounging on my couch brings me as close to a lump in my throat as I want to feel.

I've gone years without having a woman in my apartment for any length of time. I've avoided all sincere relationships. The unfamiliar warmth in my chest excites and terrifies me.

Gina spends a few nights a week here, and when she's not around, I stare at her stash of ginger ale in my fridge and refold her pajamas in my drawer.

It's a little creepy.

She's thumbing through her textbook with one hand and sketching with the other.

"Can I see?" I stride over to her and sit down, causing her sketchpad to shift.

She flashes a fierce snarl, and then her features relax.

"Whoa. That was a sharp feeling." She rests her hand on her heart.

"Yeah. Looked like you were going to bite my

head off."

She giggles and can't stop. Her textbook falls to the ground.

Her unpredictable moods no longer disturb me, but they still confuse me.

"Phew. It's so funny how I can love you, and then have an instant of hating you." Her smile is wide and her eyes glitter with delight.

"Hating me?"

"Sure—when you jostled my sketchpad, I hated you for a brief moment."

"You're right, I guess." I rub a finger along the collar of her shirt. "Most people would never admit to that sort of feeling. But I think it's true. You can have all these conflicting emotions about people you love, and still love them."

Gina shrugs and goes back to work. Discovering her emotions is both fascinating to her and ordinary. Each new revelation intrigues her. And yet she doesn't seem amazed that she needs to have these revelations.

But she amazes me.

I drag my hand away from the silky skin of her neck to open my laptop.

Scrolling through the emails, I find messages about the exchange rates.

I take a deep breath. I don't mind explaining these things to people, but you'd think they'd get it the first time around. But that's my job—analyst.

There's no point in compiling these reports if no one can read them.

I craft a few responses.

"You're huffing and puffing." Gina eyes me from behind a veil of her curls, which have fallen over the side of her face.

"I'm having trouble explaining the impact of changes in exchange rates on the value of free cash flow to the traders."

"Well, that's hard to understand. I think that article by Firestone explained it best. You showed that one to me. Why don't you send it to the traders?"

"You're a genius. You know that?"

She considers this and chews her bottom lip. "There are all kinds of intelligence. I have a few kinds. I can design a room, do complicated addition in my head, and understand financial markets. But I'll never have what you have, Chris."

"I was just sitting here, admiring how bright you are. How hard you work. And how you are so brave in this journey of revealing your emotions. What could I possibly have that you don't?"

"Charm." The corner of her mouth turns up. "I've seen you talk with people. You can converse easily with the waitress at the Chinese restaurant, even though she doesn't speak much English. You cope with my nonna's gruff manner. You have always had a ton of friends. And from what I can tell, you were able to charm many women into bed with no promise of any further dates."

My tongue sticks to the roof of my mouth. A jumble of words bombard my brain, but nothing coherent emerges.

Just a babble of defensive sounds.

"It's okay. I know it was all before we met. And I admire you for it. I would give up some of my ability in math to be able to walk into a room full of people with the confidence that comes second nature to you. And what I wouldn't do to have your ability to attract the opposite sex. Who knows? Maybe if I was able to charm men that way, I would have had a parade of them in and out of my bed."

This doesn't help clear the confusion in my mind.

"What?" is the only thing I manage to squeak out that is an actual word.

"Relax. I'm not going to do that. But I do like sex, and can see the attraction of having lots of it with different people."

"I'm not sure whether to be turned on or concerned."

"How about turned on?" She places her book and sketchpad on the coffee table, gently removes my computer from my lap, and slithers over to me.

"I think I can do turned on."

Chapter 16

CHRIS

The sharp wind cuts through my jacket. Even the Sunday morning sun can't warm the air. I stomp my feet on Gina's stoop to keep the blood flowing. Finally, Gina's grandmother opens the door.

"I guess you should wait inside. If you can't afford a decent coat for November, you can warm yourself with my heating bill."

"Thanks, Nonna Giancarlo." I step past her into the living room.

"Humph." She clomps into the kitchen and returns with a rosary and a saint's medal. I can't tell which one. Probably the patron saint of vulnerable granddaughters going to meet their boyfriend's family. She slips them both into Gina's purse resting on the entryway table. She eyes me, and if she were a *strega* from Sicily, I couldn't be more scared.

"My name's Abate," she grumbles. "Giancarlo was that no-good father of hers."

Gina descends the steps. She wears a blue skirt that hugs her hips and flares out. Her tight t-shirt is covered by a modest jacket.

"The priest at Our Lady of Peace doesn't give communion right," Nonna Abate mutters.

"Nonna, they all do it the same. I'll be back at Saint John's next week." She pecks her grandmother on the cheek. "Send my love to Aunt Sophia and the rest."

"I'm sure they made food for you. It will go to waste."

"Wrap it up and bring it home for me." Gina lifts an overnight bag. "I'm spending the evening in the city with Chris so I can go to class first thing in the morning. I'll be home tomorrow night."

Her grandmother crosses herself and mumbles a prayer.

"Bye, Nonna," Gina says pointedly, and takes my arm.

"Good-bye, Mrs. Abate. Have a good Sunday."

"Peace be with you," she snaps in the least peaceful way possible.

Gina nearly skips down the steps and scoots into the waiting car.

I give the driver directions to the church.

"We'll meet everyone there and then have dinner after."

Gina tackles me and plants a kiss on my mouth. Whenever we meet and have our first kiss of the day, it's just like our very first kiss, sending my dreams to places I never thought they'd go. Damn, she's got things stirring inside my heart and my pants.

I pull back to take her in.

"Wow. You're not nearly as nervous as I am." I stroke her hair.

"Are you kidding? I'm a fucking wreck."

I gasp. "Did Gina Giancarlo just drop the F-bomb?"

She shoots me a saucy leer. "I have a lot of years of lost cursing to make up for." She straightens her skirt. "That was all an act with Nonna. I don't want her to worry any more than she already is. I figure if I pretend meeting an army of Rinaldis is no big deal, she'll feel better about it."

"I don't think you'll ever stop amazing me." I drape an arm around her shoulder. "I wish I could be as charitable as you. I nearly reached through the phone last night to throttle my brother."

"Why?" She snuggles against me.

"He was obviously appointed by Momma to make one more attempt to dissuade me from bringing you."

"Maybe we should wait. Maybe your family needs more time."

"The sun will go supernova before they're ready." I rub her arm. "No, better to pull off the Band-Aid quick. The sooner they come face-to-face with you, the sooner they'll realize that you are just a normal girl."

"But I'm not—"

"Don't start that again. I showed them the

coroner's report. They know it wasn't your fault. They are going to have to accept that it was one of those accidents. Yes, I should have made sure Carina was out of the water. But with the lifeguards assuring me and shooing me out of the pool, what was I supposed to do?" I take a shaky breath. "I'm learning to live with it. They have to as well."

The traffic isn't heavy up to Our Lady, but they've closed off the street, as is usual on a Sunday. Even if the attendees have tapered off, no one is giving up those police barriers.

"We're here," I say.

"It's a good thing I didn't eat this morning. I think I might vomit. And there is no skill for apologizing for puking on your boyfriend's mother."

"Just don't puke up the communion wafer, and you'll be fine."

"Ha ha," she says drily.

I take her hand, and we exit the car a few blocks away. Gina nearly runs to keep pace with me. The icy wind has picked up. We don't want to be outside any longer than we need to, plus we can hear the processional hymn starting.

Dashing into the church, we pause to give our eyes time to adjust. But I know the way to the Rinaldis' usual pew. I guide Gina to where my family sits. Marco shoves over to make room. I seat Gina between him and me.

She gives a polite nod and smile. Her skills list

must be ticking like mad inside her brain. I'm sure she's running through each step twice. Marco is a gentleman, especially in church. He offers his hand, and they shake. A rush of air leaves my lungs.

At least we got off to a good start.

GINA

I manage to keep the host down and make it to the pew without hurling. I steal a few glances at Mrs. Rinaldi as she sits ramrod straight, eyes never leaving the pulpit or the choir. She doesn't even need to consult the hymnal for this week's psalm, Psalm 51 on forgiveness. There must be someone up there with a sense of humor.

When mass is over, I go down my mental list of how I want to greet Chris's family.

But I don't get a chance. There's so much commotion and jostling to get out of the pew and down the street that Chris takes my elbow and steers me around the throng of family.

Cars appear at the corner and Mrs. Rinaldi, Chris's sisters, and a few of the younger kids hop in.

Chris and I fall into a brisk step with Rico. The three blocks to his house could leave us with frostbite.

"It's nice to finally meet you, Gina. Chris has told us a lot about you."

"It's nice to meet you, too. Chris says lots of

great things about his family."

"No he doesn't, but it's good of you to try to cover for the ass."

I don't have a response to that, but Chris laughs, so I do as well. Crud. Being nervous takes away a lot of the medicine's effect.

"How are the kids?" Chris asks.

"Fine. I'm not supposed to say anything — my wife says it's too soon — but there's another on the way."

"Congratulations," I offer.

"Thanks. Another blessing, another mouth." He slaps Chris on the back. "You're the only one not continuing the bloodline."

"I see it as my service to humanity."

"What about you, Gina? You're not going to try to tie the ball and chain on the prodigal son? Get him to change his wayward ways?"

"I uh…" *No, back, please don't start itching.*

"Cool it, Rico." Chris smiles, but the cold edge to his voice runs right along with the frost in the air.

We climb the steps to his family's house, and without thinking, I pause. My gaze goes to the house three lots down. I didn't expect the flood of emotions. I still can't predict my feelings. Can anyone?

That house is where I grew up. I don't have any emotional memories associated with it. Only now, looking back, it's terribly sad. An autistic girl with a mother who could never accept her needs, and thus never met them. A vague father who vanished sometime when the girl was ten. A girl desperate for the world to see that she was indeed smart, that she could be independent. But she had no way to communicate her desires.

"You okay?" Chris kneads my shoulder.

"Yeah." I nod and follow him inside.

Background buzzing is punctuated with occasional shouts above the constant chatter. The heat is either turned way up, or the density of bodies has generated an oven-like atmosphere. I must shed my coat, but there's no place to hang it or put it. Too many people.

"Come on, let's say hi." Chris takes me to the inner sanctum of every Italian home, the kitchen.

Mrs. Rinaldi is overseeing the meal preparations.

"Momma, say hello to Gina."

The shouts end and the buzzing dies down.

The absence of noise is almost more disturbing than the assault on my senses before.

"Mrs. Rinaldi. Thank you so much for having me over. It's really a pleasure to meet you."

"We've already met. You did grow up down the street." The pause is unbearable. "Christopher, take the woman's coat. Can't you see she's dying of the heat? For crying out loud, I've raised you to treat a lady better than that."

And just like that, the chaos picks up where it

left off. Chris beams at me. I interpret all this to mean that I am tolerated, if not accepted. And that's all I think I can hope for at this point.

We spend some time visiting with the nieces and nephews. I still find relating to kids easier. They say what they think and feel. They don't use backhanded compliments or sarcasm.

"Should I help in the kitchen?" I whisper to Chris.

"I don't think you've reached that level yet. Why don't we visit with my dad?"

He leads me to the back porch. Mr. Rinaldi sits on a wicker chair, staring out into the yard.

"Pop? I want you to meet my girlfriend."

My heart bumps against my throat. It's the first time Chris has referred to me as his girlfriend since we arrived at the church.

"Hello, Mr. Rinaldi." I take the seat on the far side of him, and Chris lowers himself onto a creaky stool on the near side.

"He doesn't respond much," Chris whispers.

"I can hear you," Mr. Rinaldi snaps, and trains his eyes on me. "Who are you?"

"I'm Regina Giancarlo. I used to live down the street."

"The slow one?"

"Pop."

"Yes, I was the slow one." I giggle. "I've gotten a lot faster."

I reach out. His broad hand rests on the arm of his chair. I keep my hand steady for almost a minute until he takes it.

His grip is strong. And if his mind hadn't left, he could be tossing his grandkids up in the air and catching them in a tight embrace.

Instead, he clutches my hand as if he is slipping off the edge of a cliff and I'm his last chance at life.

"Where's Joe?"

"He's...not here, Pop."

"My brother is always too busy chasing girls to come over."

Chris takes a deep inhale. "Uncle Joe died about four years ago."

"Don't give me that nonsense. He was here last month for Carina's first communion."

Chris presses his hands on his knees and draws in a deep breath. I shake my head at him.

"Was it a nice party?" I ask Mr. Rinaldi. There's no point in explaining to him that his daughter died.

"Of course. Do you think I would skimp on my *princessa's* party?" His voice has lost the gruffness, but his mouth is still set in a firm line. "She's gone," he says quietly.

"You miss her," I say.

"Yes."

Chris's torso starts to shake, and he doesn't even try to stop the tears.

This is my moment to be strong. To cope with

the emotions around me. Not long ago, I couldn't even understand my own feelings. But now is the time I need to not only understand the emotions of others, but help them sort them out.

Mr. Rinaldi glances at Chris and starts frantically tapping his foot. The devastation will overwhelm him.

"Did you ever sing to her?" I take my free hand and stroke his wrist. The skin is soft but the hair is wiry. When Chris is as old as his father, will his wrist feel the same way? Will he have wrinkles around his eyes from squinting into the sun while he played with kids?

"'You Are My Sunshine,'" Mr. Rinaldi croaks.

I hum the familiar tune and inch closer to him. He stops tapping his foot and relaxes back into the chair. His breathing becomes even and his mouth softens. Not a smile, but the scowl is erased.

Chris has gotten his sobs under control and wipes away the streaks of tears from his face.

This is the most empowered I have ever felt in my life. And the most at ease. We stay arm to arm, grasping each other's hands. Holding on to what bit of our minds we can. Because we both understand what it's like to live with a different kind of brain.

"Gina, would you like to help set the table?" Mrs. Rinaldi's voice carries from inside.

Chris turns a million-watt smile on me. I've calmed his father, and his mother is allowing me access to the china. I might just fit in after all.

I'm humming the last chorus of the song when I'm interrupted by a screech.

"Stop that." Mrs. Rinaldi's voice has gone from high-pitched to booming. "How dare you sing him that song? What are you trying to do?"

"Momma, it was helping him calm down." Chris leaps to his feet and stands between his mother and the back of his father's chair.

"I knew it was a mistake." Mrs. Rinaldi shakes.

I extract my hand from Mr. Rinaldi's grip. I lay my hand on his shoulder and take a place beside Chris.

"Chris, we should go."

"No. I'm not leaving until she realizes that you were being kind to him. That you're not someone she can treat like a criminal."

"Chris." I take his elbow. We maneuver around his mother in the doorway.

"Are you just going to run off again?" Mrs. Rinaldi snorts.

Chris stiffens and shakes my hand off.

"Chris, buddy. Calm down." Marco comes forward and tries to step between Chris and his mother.

"Move it." Chris pushes Marco aside and steps forward. "Momma, I did some unforgivable things. I abandoned the family. And you can continue to punish me for that. But I've decided that six years of punishing myself is enough."

"Come on, Chris, it's Sunday. Let's just all sit down." Marco's smile is strained.

"But something I would never forgive myself for..." Chris's voice shakes. "I would never forgive myself for allowing you to treat Gina poorly. She's brilliant, brave, and beautiful. And if you can't find it in your heart to welcome her here, then I'm not welcome either."

He takes my hand and nearly twists my wrist as he directs us out.

A crowd of Rinaldis has blocked the passage to the front door. But I keep my head up and clutch Chris's arm as we go. He flinches, and I think he might break away from me to attack one of his brothers. But we step out into the cold fall air.

Chris pulls me down the block. I stumble trying to keep pace.

He steps off the curb and nearly stands in the path of the oncoming traffic.

"We'll never find a cab here. Let's take the subway." I step into the street and try to bring him back.

"Fine," he snaps, and heads down the block to the subway station.

When we're through the turnstile and waiting for the E train to take us back to Midtown, I think I can finally get his attention. The pride I feel for him and the gratitude overwhelm me. I can't focus on those emotions now.

"Chris, your dad shouldn't be sitting there all on his own day after day."

"I know." His eyes are focused down the dark tunnel in anticipation of the train.

"Just because his mind is going doesn't mean he should be ignored." He needs to do something to help his father if the rest of the family won't.

"It's here." He steps back from the edge of the platform and the cars rattle through.

We enter the nearly empty car and sit.

As we pass through the tunnel, our faces are reflected on the opposite window. Chris's jaw is set tight and his eyes don't show any expression. The muscles in his leg and arm that are pressed against me are coiled, ready to launch.

That all makes sense, because he is angry.

It's my face that interests me. I'm frowning, there are wrinkles in my forehead, and my eyelids are turned down. I'm sad, too. I'm sad for a man I don't even know. No, that's not really it. I'm sad for Chris. I'm sad for someone I do know and love.

I'm sad because he is angry and sad. How crazy is that?

I can feel emotions about things that don't impact me at all. But they do impact me, because they impact the person I love.

Chris continues to brood.

We pull into Fifty-First Street. Wordlessly, we

get up and climb to the surface of Lexington Avenue.

I take his hand, but he doesn't give me the usual squeeze in return.

"There are programs for people with Alzheimer's. I bet I can ask Jennifer, and she'll be able to help."

"Gina." My name is more warning than endearment.

"Is this one of those times when I should keep my thoughts to myself? I only want to make things better. So we both feel better."

He doesn't respond until we're inside his building and safely alone in the elevator to his apartment.

"You can't make it better. No one can. They live in their own world where they refuse to see reality. They refuse to see that Pop needs help. They refuse to see that they need to go to a different church because the world is changing. They refuse to accept the past. And they refuse to see that you...that you..."

The elevator doors open and I can't step off. *That I what?*

Chris gets off and looks back at me. I follow with dread of what's coming next.

He unlocks his apartment door and as soon as it's closed he hurls his keys to the floor.

"They can't see what a wonderful, brave, and loving person you are." His voice is ragged and clipped, but the mass of lead that was in my gut disappears.

Now all that exists is his kiss on my lips.

Part of me wants to ask more about what he means, but the other part is focused on his hands and how he accomplished shedding his coat and mine while our lips were locked together.

And now his hands rip apart my blouse. For a moment I think about the cost, but when his head dips and he runs his tongue along the edge of my lacy bra, I don't care.

He guides me to his bedroom, kicking off his shoes as we go.

"I want you so bad." His breath flutters the hair around my ear, and it sends a tremor to my belly.

"Me too," is all I can say.

We strip with a frantic need, trying to maintain contact while flinging clothes to the side.

We fall onto his bed, and the warm, hard muscles of his legs bear down on my body. There's nothing I want more than to be trapped under him.

I know what I want now, and what he wants as well.

He sits up long enough to look at me. It's painstaking the way he trails his hand over my body, lightly brushing against my breast and unsettling my composure. I can't think when his fingers work magic. I need to learn to get my brain offline.

He makes it easy when his kisses move from my

mouth, and his tongue stakes a trail down to where he can give me the most pleasure.

I hear my voice squeal. The brush of his tongue is nearly unbearable as I reach the crest of orgasm.

I must have gone offline, because after the waves subside, Chris is nuzzling my neck.

I wrap my arms around his back and press him into me.

"Condom," he gasps before we go further.

When he reaches to his side table, the chill of the air that is not warmed by his body drifts over my skin. I never want to feel that chill again. I want only Chris-warmed space around me.

He enters me with a sigh of relief.

I wind my legs behind him and tilt just so he hits all the right spots.

"I love you," I whisper in his ear. "Really, it's love."

"I know it is. I can feel it." The last words are grunts against what I can tell is his building pressure.

"Go on," I urge him.

His pace increases, and the slap of our bodies lets me know that I am able to make love like any woman.

Because it is love.

Chapter 17

CHRIS

Gina is going to love our plans for tonight. I want her birthday celebration to be something she remembers forever. And forever is something I've been thinking about.

Her grandmother opens the door and waves me inside.

"Hello, Mrs. Abate."

"Gina is still upstairs getting ready." She plods to her easy chair and sits down. She is wearing her church dress and places her black patent leather purse on her knees.

"May I?" I indicate the couch.

She shrugs, folds her hands across her lap, and stares. Like a lioness who is confident she can catch her prey, there's no need to hurry or make the first move.

"Mrs. Abate, can I speak with you?"

"It's better than sitting in silence."

"I have very strong feelings for Gina." I sit forward and rest my forearms on my knees. "Gina feels the same way about me. And I'm hoping that we'll continue to have strong feelings for each other."

"They didn't teach you to speak clearly at college?" Her eyes shoot laser beams at me.

"It's difficult, what I want to ask you." I rub my palms on my pants.

"If you mean it, then it shouldn't be difficult."

"You're right." I take a deep breath. "If I were to ask Gina to marry me, would you give us your blessing? You're important to Gina, and I hope you understand, that means you're important to me."

A door opens upstairs. "Is that you, Chris?" Gina calls.

"Yeah." My voice cracks like a twelve-year-old's. I'm not ready for Gina to come down and hear this, and her nonna is still giving me the stink eye.

"I'll be down in a minute." The door closes again, and Mrs. Abate still stares at me.

"I think I spoke plainly enough." I find some courage. "We don't need your permission, but with my family basically kicking me to the curb, I'd hope that if we do have a future together, Gina's family will be included."

She shakes her head. "How can parents do that to their kids? What would a child have to do to make a parent not want to see them?" She wrings her hands. "Gina's mother left because... Well, even then I would have taken my daughter back. Even after she proved herself to be a terrible mother, I would have taken her back. That's what it means to be a parent."

She shakes a finger at me. "I won't let anyone abandon her again. She's been hurt enough."

"I would never do that. If I make a commitment to her, it would be for life."

"No matter what? No matter if this drug stops working and she…she goes back…"

I swallow. That isn't a scenario I ran through. I imagined what would happen if I lost my job and didn't have enough money to support a family. I considered what would happen if my family never came around. The possibility that Gina might break up with me crossed my mind. But her state as it is now—I took for granted that she'd stay this way.

"She's a smart woman, and I have faith that she'll be fine," I answer.

"But if she's not…" Her voice wavers. "Because you've been known to run off when things get difficult."

She's testing me. Goading me into disappearing like I did before.

"I would never leave Gina because of her autism. I've seen what it's like when the people you love reject you. Yes, I've been the rejecter in the past. But recently, I've been on the other side. I've grown up."

She smiles a thin-lipped grin and places a hand over mine. "No rush. Eh?"

"Okay, Mrs. Abate. No rush."

Gina descends the steps. Man, her curvy legs

and hips are hugged by an electric-blue skirt, and a plunging white top creates an amazing contrast to her chestnut hair and sea-green eyes. She looks good in white. A swell forms in my chest, and a flutter in my gut. I just hope her nonna doesn't notice the shift in my pants.

"What?" Gina's brows knit together. "I think something was happening here while I was upstairs."

"What would be happening here?" her grandmother replies.

"You're right, Gina. Trust your instincts. You've caught on to the awkward silence that occurs when people are having a deep conversation, and the subject of that conversation enters the room."

"I knew it." She hops. "Wait. I should be angry or upset that you were talking about me while I wasn't here."

"No, you should be honored." I take her coat off the hook and hold it out to help her into it. It's an old gray coat, and the sleeves are frayed, but it was expensive, once.

She shrugs into it, and I have a nice view down the front as I help her.

I catch her grandmother's glare and try my best boyish, charming grin. She isn't impressed.

I repeat the process with her scarf. Another sensible wool item.

"I think you two will enjoy this." I hold Nonna's

elbow as we descend the stoop and I help her into the car service sedan.

"A lot of fuss for a birthday," she grumbles.

Gina gives me a thumbs-up behind her back, and I brace myself for a night of jumping through Nonna's hoops.

GINA

Nonna sits ramrod straight as the car passes over the bridge, and we enter Manhattan.

"Where are we going?" I ask, and pat Chris's knee. I'm squished between him and Nonna, which is probably a good thing. The tension between them was thick. Amazing that I can sense that. Even though I have no idea what they were discussing, I know they were at odds.

"It's a surprise. But I think you'll both like it."

"It will be a lovely evening." Nonna grimaces, and I take it for what it's worth.

I might have an inkling as to what they were talking about. It was me, and Nonna was probably grilling him on not running off or cheating, or any of the other terrible things she thinks he is capable of doing. I'll always be her little girl who needs protection. And part of me is relieved that she wants to take care of me. But the other part is furious that she thinks I still need taking care of. Her mind-set might not change, even if I do.

We pull up to the restaurant, and Chris gives instructions to the driver to return in two hours.

"What is this place?" Nonna squints at the building.

"It's a supper club." Chris offers his arm to Nonna. She regards it and accepts it by linking her arm through his.

Inside, the lights are dim and café tables ring a small stage. The hostess takes us to a booth with a high back at the edge of the room.

I position myself between them, again hoping that Nonna didn't ask him anything too personal and that Chris managed to keep his cool.

"We'll take three ginger ales," Chris tells the waitress before she has a chance to hand out cocktail menus.

"What happens here?" Nonna nods to the stage.

"You'll see." Chris looks over the menu. "Mrs. Abate, do you see anything you'd like?"

"The lasagna is probably mushy."

"Then get the chicken," I suggest.

But when the waitress returns with our drinks to take our order, Nonna asks for the lasagna, and Chris and I follow her. It might be my birthday, but this is really about getting Nonna to accept Chris.

"This is a great place. Isn't it a great place, Nonna? When was the last time we were at such a fancy place?"

She shrugs and arranges her napkin.

The lights dim further and the spotlight comes on the stage. A piano player and drummer hop on.

An unseen announcer welcomes us to the supper club and calls up the first act. One of the waiters puts down his order pad and takes the stage.

This first act is a medley of Broadway hits, and I know Nonna knows most of the songs, because she gets the soundtracks to the major shows. I hold my breath. *Please let her posture ease. Please let her enjoy tonight. Please let her approve of my relationship with Chris.*

Our salads come and another server takes the stage. This one sings Beatles songs, and Nonna concentrates on her food.

"Is it good?" Chris asks her.

"Yes, well. It's hard to mess up a salad. The lettuce is fresh. I'll give them that."

Chris grinds his teeth, and I beg him with my eyes for more patience. His frown tells me he's been trying all night to be cordial, and Nonna hasn't returned the sentiment.

A few more performers get on stage, and I notice Nonna tapping her fingers to the music. When she catches me staring at her hand, she folds her hands in her lap and straightens herself up again.

The entrees are really good. I don't tell Nonna that the lasagna is almost as good as hers.

"This is much better than I thought it would be."

Chris opens his mouth, and I expect some

snarky remark is about to come out. I shake my head, and he takes a deep breath.

"Excuse me." Chris places his napkin on the table and heads toward the restroom.

"Nonna," I snap. "Would it kill you to be kind to Chris? He's gone out of his way to plan a nice evening for us."

"And he has plans for just you later." She dabs the corner of her mouth.

"This can't be news to you. I've been sleeping with him for months."

"But this is your birthday. He wants to whisk you away tonight, and I suppose I'll ride home by myself in that car with too much air freshener."

It's not just that I'm moving on and developing new relationships. Nonna's main purpose has been to take care of me, and soon she might not have that.

"Nonna, I will always need you. Our lives will always be entwined." I pull her to me, and her tiny shoulder nestles under my arm.

"Chris is a good boy," she says, pulling away. "But the man you end up with has to be exceptional."

"I won't settle for less. But you need to trust that I can discern who is exceptional and who is not."

Nonna's words are cut off when Chris returns.

"I told the waitress three tiramisus. I hope that's okay." He slides in next to me.

"That's my favorite," Nonna says casually, and

keeps her eyes on the stage.

The bartender, a large man with a full beard, approaches the microphone. Accompanied by the piano, he launches into some of Nonna's favorite Italian opera pieces for tenors.

She shuts her eyes and sways to the music. A soft smile graces her lips.

Chris's mouth drops open, and he turns to me for clarification.

"You should've had them lead with the opera," I whisper.

Nonna comes back to the present when they place her dessert in front of her.

"You know what goes good with tiramisu? A nice sambuca."

Chris waves the waitress over and orders two sambucas.

"To your health." He raises his glass to Nonna.

"And to yours." She returns the salute. They clink glasses for a fraction of a moment. But that's the moment I want to hold on to. The two most important people in my life, on the same team. My team.

Chapter 18

GINA

A sleepover party is something most girls take for granted. They'll go to at least one or two in their adolescence.

The time I slept at my cousin's house doesn't count. Yes, I brought a sleeping bag and placed it neatly on the floor parallel to her bed. But the only reason I was there was because my mother had a job doing hair in Atlantic City. At least that's what she told me. Looking back, I think she just wanted a night away. And I can't blame her.

It couldn't have been easy for a single mother to care for a kid like me.

Sarah flings open her front door and yells, "Hey, birthday girl."

"Hi." I step inside. I've been to Sarah's apartment in Brooklyn once before. The last time she had a party, I spent the evening trying to convince her to move her furniture and showing her pictures of design ideas on my phone.

Her place is still a design nightmare, but I know to keep it to myself.

"It's really nice of you to have me and Franny

over."

"Are you kidding? It's been weeks since Chad moved out. I need to change the energy of this place, and a slumber party for your birthday is just the thing."

Her buzzer sounds again, and she opens the door. I introduce Franny, who carries a sleeping bag and pillow.

"I didn't bring anything but my change of clothes," I say. There must be some unwritten code of what to do and how to behave at sleepovers. I never read that memo.

"I've got plenty of stuff."

Sarah gets beers, and I take one tiny sip. It's musky and bitter. Even if I were allowed to drink, I can't see myself ever wanting a beer.

Franny has a small gift bag. "I know you said no gifts, but it's your birthday."

The pink bag stuffed with tissue paper weighs down my arm when I take it.

"Really?"

"What's a party without gifts?"

I pull out the tissue paper and find a new sketchpad and the high-end pencils the bookstore sells. The ones I bypassed for the cheaper brand.

"Oh, Franny."

"Zack chipped in, too. We saw you gaze longingly at them. Your sketches are beautiful and deserve some nice materials."

"Thanks. I didn't expect this."

"Then you certainly aren't expecting this." Sarah hands me a tiny black gift bag that is so light there can't be anything it in.

"Go on." Sarah nudges me.

I reach in and can't find anything but more tissue paper. Then my finger hooks around a strap of something. When I remove my hand, a lace thong dangles at the end.

I flip through a list of responses in my mind. Somehow, the "expressing thanks" skill I learned at the center doesn't seem appropriate.

"I bet you've got nothing sexy to wear for Chris when you're in bed." Sarah slaps me on the back.

"We usually don't wear anything when we're in bed."

Franny laughs so hard her beer sputters from her mouth. "That's what I like about you, Gina. You're so forthright."

"Yeah." I fidget with the thong.

"That's what we all like about Gina." Sarah gives me an exaggerated nod. She knows Franny doesn't know I have autism.

"Thanks for the gifts, really. This might be the best birthday I've ever had."

"Oh, then we have to set the bar even higher." Franny pulls out DVDs of romance movies, and Sarah lays out the Chinese food she ordered.

I get a glimpse of what it's like to be one of the

girls. Sarah offers to paint my toenails, and Franny sprawls on the couch as we watch a movie.

There's a camaraderie I used to notice. Girls would walk together, or sit together, and their bodies were relaxed and at ease. I can remember watching this, but now I feel the connection to other people. An intimate connection that's a different kind from a Chris-intimacy.

"He's so hot." Sarah nods at the latest celebrity on the television.

"I wouldn't kick him out of bed for eating crackers," Franny agrees.

We giggle. This is my remedial course in girlfriends. I'm healing from the lack of friendships and intimacy from the early part of my life.

"Gina, stop drooling over the dude on TV. Your phone keeps buzzing."

"Oh, sorry." I gingerly get up and mince around the debris of cookie packages and nail polish. The screen says it's Nonna.

"Hi, Nonna, are you okay?"

"Gina *mia*, you left your pills here. What are you going to do in the morning?" The panic in her voice isn't necessary to send my own heart rate through the red zone.

"I, uh...uh." Sarah and Franny are staring at me with questioning gazes. "Uh." Fear grips my chest. Not only do I have no idea what to do about missing a pill in the morning and what effect that might have on me, or the study, but I also have to figure out something to say to my friends. Something to explain the horror that must be on my face.

"Gina, aren't you going to work from there tomorrow?"

"Yes." I drag out the word, hoping to buy time. I inch into the bathroom. "I need to talk to my grandmother," I say, and nearly slam the door behind me. "Nonna, what am I going to do?"

"I can get up early and meet you at the coffee shop. It will only be a few hours later than usual."

"But I can't eat before I take it. And what am I going to say to Sarah about not eating breakfast? She's going to make pancakes. And how are we going to explain you coming to the coffee shop?"

"Then come home. Wake up very early and come to Queens and go back."

"What excuse do I give for that?

Nonna is quiet. "Maybe you should tell them."

"No way. We're having a good time. A regular fun time, like regular girls."

"Can Chris help?"

"He does know I'm taking medicine and part of a study." I tap the edge of the sink. "It's a lot to ask of him. To go all the way to our house and then drop it off here."

"He says he loves you."

"I can't see any other way. Okay, I'll call him and let you know." I end the call and text Chris.

Me: *Are you busy?*

Chris: *No. Are you having fun at your slumber party?*

Me: *Yes, but I have a huge favor to ask.*

Chris: *Anything.*

Me: *I left my pills at home. I need to take them first thing in the morning before I eat. I don't want anyone to know about them.*

There's a long pause, and I guess he's reading or it's taking a long time for the message to go through. Maybe I asked too much.

Chris: *Should I go and pick it up and bring it to you?*

Me: *Would you? I will pay you back.*

Chris: *Babe, I can think of all sorts of ways for you to make it up to me.*

Me: *Whatever you want, stud.*

Relief washes over me. I text Nonna and tell her to expect Chris. When Chris gets to Sarah's, I'll think up some excuse to run out for ice cream.

"Everything okay?" Sarah asks as I emerge from the bathroom.

"Sorry about that. My grandmother gets nervous when I'm not at home." I flop down next to Franny.

"She relies on you, huh?" Franny says. "It's nice you're there to take care of her."

Sarah's eyebrow is still raised. She knows it's more the other way around. Or at least it used to be. But she won't give away my secret.

We settle back into watching television. Franny

has put in another one of her DVDs.

I might be the luckiest girl. How many people get cured of their autism, make great friends, start an exciting career, and have a hot boyfriend who comes to their rescue?

That balloon in my chest might burst from all the wonderful feelings.

Still, the thought of getting found out hangs over me. I'm not supposed to say too much about the study. And I certainly don't want to have to tell anyone about my autism if I don't have to. Franny is my first friend who doesn't know.

I have to make sure to play it as cool as possible and keep my newfound emotions in check.

When Tom Hanks kisses Meg Ryan, I find my cheek is damp.

I swipe away the tears and try to duck my head away. I'm so lame. All these new emotions overwhelm me. I can't even watch a stupid movie without these feelings welling up and taking my control away, threatening the new friendships I'm forming.

"It gets me every time also." Franny dabs at her face with the sleeve of her pajamas.

When will I stop being amazed at emotions? Here's a perfectly normal person who cries at a movie she's seen a million times.

Maybe I'll be lucky enough to be moved to tears over and over again.

CHRIS

It's not the chill of the drizzling rain that has me hunched into my coat, as I lean against the parking meter. It's the white bottle in my pocket with the unmistakable red G with the swooping design. I shift my weight and the pills clatter inside. It can't be heard above the traffic rushing past on Sixth Avenue. But I feel the movement as if boulders are cracking against my leg.

The confirmation was almost a relief, to rid myself of the sinking feeling in my gut since Gina texted me. Now, I know for sure that Gina is part of the Genloran study.

I was skirting the edge of the law by using my frat buddy's intel, but now...

Even though I made the recommendations before I knew Gina, it could look bad. Scratch that — I've always known Gina. Since we were babies, we lived next door to each other.

Who could say we didn't stay in touch? My family still lives in the same house.

A cab cuts the corner tight and splashes New York City puddle water onto my shoes. I barely flinch.

"Chris," Gina calls as she emerges from Sarah's building. She waves, and her face is bright with birthday joy.

"Hey." I straighten myself and take her in my arms. I rest my chin on her head and let her curls jiggle against my neck.

"Mmmm. You feel good." She looks up, and the light glistens in her green eyes.

"What did you tell them?" I release her, reluctant to let go of the comfort her body brings.

"I said that it wasn't a party without Oreos, and they agreed. I insisted they did enough for me, so I've got to pray that bodega has Oreos." She stamps her feet to warm up. "I've never lied like that before. In fact, I can't remember lying ever. It doesn't feel good."

"Nope, lying never feels good. But sometimes you have to." I reach into my pocket and yank out the pill bottle. "Here."

"Thanks." She tucks it into her coat. "Doesn't that mean it's wrong? If lying always feels bad, doesn't that mean you shouldn't do it?"

I can't look her in the eye anymore. I train my gaze on the flashing light of the Chinese takeout place. "Why did you lie to your friends?"

"To protect myself, I guess. I'm not ready to share with Franny that I'm autistic. And I probably shouldn't tell Sarah about the drug study. I guess that's protecting her and the drug company. I probably shouldn't have even told you." She laughs and winds her arm around my waist.

"I guess that's why people lie, to protect

themselves and others." I work to accept the solace her arm should bring, but it's not there.

"Do you lie?" Her expression shifts into investigation mode, when she's trying to study the human condition and for some warped reason is using me as a normative data point.

"Everyone does. But only when I need to."

"To protect yourself?"

"And those I love." I kiss her. Her lips taste like corn chips.

"I'd better buy some Oreos." She bobs on her toes. "I don't know how to thank you for this." She pats her coat and the pills rattle.

"I'll think of something you can do in return." I paste on my game face, which right now is another kind of lie.

CHRIS

The green velvet ripples against her hip. Gina is the hottest girl in the room.

I take her by the elbow and steer her to the bar.

The past month has been a sprint toward relationship land. I've successfully blocked out all conscious knowledge of Gina's medication. And she has become more in touch with her consciousness. Not quite self-conscious, just self-aware. We spend so much time together that I almost forget what it was like to be single. I remember just enough to know I don't want to be single again. And I'm finding I like a girl with depth. Who knew?

"Ginger ale?" I ask.

"Yes, please." She turns to face the ballroom.

The Humbolt and Sutter holiday party is as extravagant as it is ridiculous.

The tuxes and gowns are meant to show off all the wealth that we have accumulated over the year. The competition doesn't end, even for a party that's supposed to be fun.

And even though I don't go to church and have few fond memories of my Catholic schooling, I can't help but cringe when I think about what the holidays are meant to be about.

"Isn't that your boss?" Gina tilts her head toward the dance floor.

Breckner stutter-steps around the floor with his wife, who is wearing a sequined dress that's nearly blinding.

"Not bad for a guy his age." I drink my martini and watch Gina watching the crowd.

Her face has a relaxed quality. Her stunning features no longer wrinkle in confusion or deep thought every moment. Now, she takes it all in, processes it at a speed Rob could never hope to achieve.

"Penny for your thoughts." I guide her to a table, and we sit. Her shapely calves peep from between the slit on the side of her dress.

"I was wondering if you were going to ask me to dance." She smiles, and her parted lips distract me from remembering this is a professional work party.

Too entranced to follow through, I stare at her face, which does start to collapse in concern.

"You don't think I can dance like that, huh?" The old concern creases her forehead.

"Gina, you can do anything you put your mind to. Don't for a second doubt my belief in you." I stand and offer her my hand.

Her heels aren't stiletto or platform, so she doesn't measure up to the height of the other women. But she stands taller in bravery, intelligence, and sexiness (even if she is short).

We glide around the floor. Luckily, the mandatory social dance class in high school stuck with me. It kills me to keep my hand on her waist and not let it wander where it wants to go.

Gina closes her eyes, allows me to lead her, and lets the music hum through her body.

"Rinaldi, you brought that charming young woman with you." Breckner and his wife stop by us.

We halt in our dancing, pulled out of the trance and back into work mode.

"Bob, this is Gina."

"Let's get some drinks." Bob directs us to a table and signals a waiter with a tray of champagne flutes.

Gina delicately takes one, and barely tips it against her lips. She places her glass near mine on the table. I'll drink some of hers so it looks like she's had some.

"Gina, I'm afraid the boys will talk shop," Mrs. Breckner says with a knowing smile.

"That's okay. I was mulling over an article Chris gave me on balancing derivatives and futures." She places her hand on my arm. "Mr. Breckner, did you read that article?"

Bob takes off with his pompous voice on how the risk adverse and new federal regulations are strangling business. I half listen, because I know there will be a quiz, but Gina nods and throws in a few "ahs" here and there.

I sit a little straighter and place my arm around her shoulder.

"And you want to be an interior designer?" Breckner shakes his head.

"You should see how she transforms a room." I squeeze her shoulder, and color flushes her face and neck.

"I can already see that." Mrs. Breckner's wry smile is as much for her husband as for us. "Gina, careful or you'll take over this company, not just one of Bob's brightest associates."

"I have no intention of taking over anything." Gina looks up into my eyes. "Well, except for Chris's apartment. The furnishings are all wrong."

GINA

The evening spins by. We dance, we drink, we talk.

It's the first time I have ever been to a real party and felt comfortable. Chris smiles all night. The trauma with his parents still hangs over us, but he seems to forget it tonight. Ever since that night he's been distracted. Not from me, but I can tell his mind is whirling and he's thinking big thoughts. He has some decisions to make about how to cope with his family. Where do I fit in? Can he maintain relationships with them and with me?

It doesn't matter to me if he continues to be close to his family. I'm secure in his feelings toward me.

"Ready to go?" he whispers in my ear.

"People haven't started to leave yet." I scan the room and the party is still going strong.

"But I want you to myself." His words send shivers up my back.

Good shivers that let me know I'll enjoy what's to come.

"If you think it's okay to leave this early." I wink. Winking is a good way of flirting. I've always been able to wink, but now I know when to use it.

Chris winks back, and we make the rounds saying good-bye. I endure a leer from Chris's friend Rob. That guy is a creep. He sees women as good for blowjobs and fetching drinks. I'm so glad I can see things like that now, and respond with an offended expression. Not that he'd pick up on it. You don't have to be autistic to be clueless.

The air outside is cold, but there's no wind as we exit the hotel.

"Wanna walk off some of that champagne? It's only ten blocks to my place," Chris says.

"Yes. And let's go down Fifth Avenue." I've seen the shops and Rockefeller Center decorated for the holidays before. But late at night with Chris's arm through mine, it's not just dazzling, it's magical.

"Thanks for coming tonight. I know parties aren't your thing." Chris kisses the top of my head.

"They might become my thing." With Chris covering for my ginger ale preference, and as long as the conversations stay on finance and interior design, I think I can pass. "Zack and Franny are having a New Year's party. Won't be nearly as fancy as tonight's…"

"If they can tolerate a financial analyst at a party for artsy types, then I'd love to go."

We stop by the closed ice rink and take in the enormous Norwegian spruce adorned with multicolored lights.

"Sit here." Chris points to a bench under an angel blowing a trumpet.

The chilly metal seeps through my coat and the green velvet dress that Sarah and I found at a consignment shop. The best thing is that I didn't spill anything on it, and I can probably sell it back for not much less than what I bought it for.

Chris shoves his hand in his pocket and fishes around for something.

"Gina, we make a good team."

"Team?"

"I mean we're good together. I want us to continue to be good together."

"Why wouldn't we?"

"I-I…" Chris stands and takes a few paces away from me. "I don't know what I'm trying to say. Except I love you." He turns back.

"I love you, too." I scramble in my head for the right response. I try to pick up on the cues of his body language. Something is troubling him, but his words are positive. If I had years of decoding people and their meaning, I might be able to guess at what he's trying to say. "Chris, did I do something wrong at the party?"

"No, sweetheart, not at all." He returns to the bench and takes my mittened hands in his fine-leather-gloved ones. "I'm just trying to say we should spend even more time together. In the future, too."

"Okay." I race through all the lessons Jennifer has gone over with me. I pick two or three things that Chris could be hinting at. "Chris, do you want…want me to move in with you?"

His posture relaxes, and he shoves his hands back into his pockets.

"I guess, yeah. I guess that's what I was getting at." His smile is sheepish but cute.

"You know Nonna would never accept that. She couldn't keep me from doing it. But I don't want to hurt her that way." I stroke his arm, which I can't feel through his heavy coat and my mitten. "But I can stay over anytime you want." I wink again, and he laughs.

"Come on, then. Let's go."

I take his hand, and we no longer stroll to admire the window displays. We practically jog to his apartment building. At each intersection, he whispers what he has planned once we get inside, and my libido is about to burst through my thinning wool coat.

He nuzzles my ear in the elevator, and I giggle.

He dashes down the hall, pulling me after him. The tension that started to build when we danced has become unbearable.

We tumble into his apartment and immediately fall onto the couch, kissing. We don't break apart to pull our coats off and fling the scarves away. He kicks his shoes off. I need to unbuckle the straps from mine. I can't do it while maintaining lip contact.

"Wait, wait." He pulls back. "Meet me in the bathroom. I have a new shower massager I want you to see."

"Oooh," I gasp. That's maybe the most intimate thing we could do, and I want to do it.

KATE FOREST

I take off my shoes and shimmy out of my stockings. The water has come on in the bathroom.

Chris is nude, his erection jutting forth. His strong arms beckon me toward him. He's lit candles, and the scent of vanilla wafts toward me. The hum of the shower beating against the tiles is loud enough to mask my nervous peep. But Chris's eyes question me.

"Is this okay?" he asks.

I nod and slip the rest of my clothes off. As I approach, the warmth of the spray flows over my skin, and I drop my arm that was covering my breasts.

Chris's lips spread into a wide grin, and he follows me into the tight space, closing the glass door.

"Here, let me." He takes a bar of soap and works it into a lather. His slippery hands travel across my shoulders and down my sides. I allow my eyes to close, and my head to rest against the cool tile, a welcome relief from the overwhelming heat.

He gets more soap and circles my breasts.

"Please, Chris, down there." I spread my legs apart, because the torture he inflicts with those sudsy fingers needs to be at my sex.

"Mmmm." He leans forward to nibble my ear, his erection pressing into my belly. And his fingers part my folds and slip around in a pattern I can't define. All I know is that the water caressing down my body, Chris's coarse chest hairs, the smooth, cool tile, and the magic of his fingers work together so that I might shoot straight into the air. The crash to the ground would be so worth it.

"Here." Chris stops and hands me the soap.

My groan reverberates off the walls of the small room, echoing my frustration. But his mischievous smirk lets me know I'll get what's mine.

"My turn to torment you."

"Yes." He places his palms flat on the wall on either side of my head.

I take my time, slowly drawing the edge of the soap up one side of his flat abs and down the other. The lather drips down over his cock, which twitches, demanding attention.

Stroking it with my slick hands, I feel the power that I have in giving him pleasure.

He grunts and pushes back. His eyes drill into me as rivulets of water run over his face.

"Gina." He leans in, and the fiercest kiss of my life lifts me onto tiptoes. I grab his shoulders so I don't slip. His tongue is frantic to reach every part of mine, and we're locked together. Until he breaks away, panting.

"How about like this?"

He turns me around, and I'm pretty sure what I need to do is bend forward a bit.

From behind, he reaches around to stimulate me while the tip of his erection parts my sex.

The tile against my face helps quell the heat as he slides ever so slowly into me.

My clit is practically singing as his pace increases. I lose my ability to tell where my body ends and his begins. The orgasm buckles my knees, and Chris steadies me as I feel him slip out.

He moans as he comes outside of me.

Wordlessly we get out and towel each other off. I shiver at the cold of the floor, but my skin is still on fire.

"Come to bed." His voice rumbles through me.

"I want to keep my phone with me in case Nonna calls."

I kiss his nose, and he rolls his eyes.

I pad into the living room, where we shed our coats. That is what sex is like for women who know what they want, with men who are considerate lovers, for couples that are as intimate as they can be. This is what a relationship is about. Being vulnerable and safe all at the same time.

I pick up our coats to hang them, and something drops.

A black velvet jewelry box tumbles next to the couch.

I freeze. I know what comes in those boxes. I smack my head. Chris was going to propose when we were sitting on that bench, and I missed it. I am an idiot. How many women would have missed those clues? None. Well, one with autism.

Then I do the cleverest thing I have ever done. I kick the box a few inches under the couch. I can pretend I never saw it, and Chris can save face about chickening out.

Now I have to decide if I'm glad he didn't follow through and force me to choose something I'm completely not ready for, or crushed that he couldn't bring himself to ask me.

Chapter 19

CHRIS

I pay the cabbie and follow him to the trunk where I dumped all the gifts.

Real greenery and white lights adorn the front of the Rinaldi house, as they have every year of my life. Momma would never use fake plants or colored lights. I have no idea why, but she turns her nose up at the neighbors and their displays.

I wonder who strung them up this year, because it certainly wasn't Pop.

I make two trips up the steps to haul the presents. When Marco finally comes to the door, snow has covered the ones on top.

"Hey, you no-good shit, you made it." He smiles and steps back to let me in.

This will be my reception from everyone this Christmas Eve. Storming out with Gina last time I was here put a chill on relations. Not as great as when Carina died, but it's opened the old wounds.

"Where's the spirit of the season?" I ask, and shove a bag into his hands. "Where's the warmth of my family's bosom?"

He rolls his eyes. "We can eat now. Chris is here," he calls into the house.

At least all my nieces and nephews come running to sort the gifts. They diligently add to the growing piles under the tree.

"Is Aunt Gina coming?" little Terry asks, examining a box.

"She's in Florida, like every year." Momma emerges from the kitchen.

"That one is for my friend, Gina." I snatch it out of Terry's hands and place it by the front door so I can take it on my way out. "Must have gotten mixed up."

Momma's lips purse like she's tasted baccalà that hasn't been soaked enough.

"Got all seven fishes, Momma?" I take her in a hug and plant a kiss on her cheek. I will kill these people with kindness if I have to drink every last drop of the god-awful eggnog my sister insists on forcing down our throats.

"Hi, Chris." Maria pecks me on the cheek. "Good thing you're alone," she whispers in my ear before releasing the hug.

"I thought we could have a merry Christmas." I nod even though I want to lecture them about welcoming people in your home, goodwill to all, even those with autism. But I keep my mouth shut. I can rise above them, do my filial duty with a smile.

"Now that you're here, we'll eat," she says.

"Bring your father to the table." Momma places another platter among the many platters.

I wind between bodies rushing for spots at the table, down the hall, and to the back porch.

Pop isn't there.

Celebrities sing carols on the television. I turn to go back to check his bedroom and movement out in the yard catches my attention.

Pop lopes in circles. He stops to scoop some snow and dump it on his head. He wears only his pants, a dress shirt Momma probably made him put on, and his house slippers.

"Pop." I dash outside and chase after him.

He's got some speed despite his age. But I grab him around the chest.

"Pop, you'll freeze out here."

"I'm having a snowball fight with Joe." Pop insists he's playing with his deceased brother. He's shivering under my arms and struggles to free himself from my hold.

"Okay, but it's time to come in and eat. It's Christmas." I pull him toward the house.

He fights me, but gives up and allows me to guide him up the back steps.

"Momma, we need some towels and a blanket," I call once we're inside.

Pop is mumbling, and I can't understand him. English mixed with Italian mixed with the confusion of dementia, through chattering teeth.

I place him in his chair and bend to remove his slippers and sopping socks. His toes are blue, and I rub them between my hands.

"Hurry." There's panic in my voice that I hope someone in the front of the house hears.

Momma arrives with assorted siblings behind her. "What's the commotion?"

"Pop decided to go outside. We need blankets and some dry clothes."

"Here, let me." Momma steps forward and takes Pop's arm. She coos softly and brings him to the bedroom.

"I can't believe she's so calm about it." I'm shaking more from fear and adrenaline than the snow melting in my loafers.

"It's not the first time he's gone outside without us noticing," Donny says.

"He could wander off anywhere." The volume I reach sends the rest of my brothers and sisters back.

"The yard is fenced in. He'd have to climb over or unlock the gate." Marco is always the go-between, the family spokesman.

"And what if he does? Marco, you know he can't stay here. Momma's getting older herself. She can't care for him."

He shrugs. "You tell her that. Besides, you don't want to see him in an institution rotting away in the corner."

"There are some nice places. Gina was telling

me —"

"I wouldn't mention her if I were you." Marco looks over his shoulder. "Since the last time you were here with her, and she tried to tell Momma how to care for Pop." He shakes his head. "Momma's more determined than ever to keep him here."

"That's nuts."

"Well, you should know nuts." He challenges me.

Rage boils in my veins. My fists clench and load my arm, ready to fight his ignorant remark.

Marco stands his ground. "You're going to take a swing? Go ahead. And then run out. Run out and abandon your family. You've got practice."

There's nothing I want to do more. Leave these people behind and get on with my life, a life with Gina, my life in the city. I spot the tracks Pop made in the snow. He needs me. If I leave now, Gina would never forgive me. She told me to make peace with them, and I will. If for no other reason than I can look her in the eye tomorrow morning and tell her I did.

"It's Christmas, Marco. Why would I punch someone on Christmas?" I slap his back harder than a friendly slap, but the message has been sent. Don't talk about Gina, and I won't make a scene while I'm here.

We join everyone at the table. Pop has changed into dry pants and a sweater. He's seated at the head, with Momma to his right.

"Chris should say Grace," Marco offers.

Momma nods. Her eyes and nose are red. No one has ever seen her cry. I heard her, after Carina was found, wailing in her room. But when she emerged, she was composed, with only the redness to give away what she endured. I suspect her grief for Pop is a quieter, more insidious grief that washes over her daily. With every time he asks for his brother, or fails to bring the fork to his lips, she grieves a bit more for their past.

I bow my head, and the prayer emanates from me without a thought. But it gives me a moment to collect myself and put on my game face. I promised Gina I'd reconnect with them.

The traditional seafood dishes are passed about, and we eat and gossip, and I'm sucked back into the fold. I can participate in the conversation without really thinking. The same topics — who in the neighborhood is moving in or out. Did you see what the Arlottis did to their yard? Have you heard about the fifth grade teacher at the school?

We linger over the meal, because we have to stay up for Midnight Mass. Dishes are slowly transported to the kitchen, where Momma directs the packing and storing of leftovers.

"Momma." I pull her to the side where there's at least the pretense of privacy. "I'm worried about Pop. Is there something I can do to help? Do you need money?"

Her back stiffens. I'm about to get a lecture. But then she shakes her head and her shoulders round. "No, Christofo. That's kind of you, but I can take care of him." She pats my back. "It's good you came home for Christmas. You make good money at your job in New York. Time to think about a family. You're my only one not settled."

"Momma, you're not going to like my answer if we talk about that."

"Bah. That girl's only a passing thing. She's someone you date, not someone you marry. If you want to marry someone from around here, there are plenty of nice girls. But I know you." She shakes her finger at me. "You'll end up with a woman from the city. Just make sure she's Catholic. Italian would be nice." She shrugs. "But I'm realistic."

I open my mouth to argue about Gina. I catch a warning look from Maria and close my mouth.

"Let's get our coats on. It will be crowded," Marco calls.

As gloves and hats are passed around, I spot Momma turning to the corner, wiping her eyes.

"Momma. You okay?"

She takes a deep breath. We all stare. Momma crying twice in one evening.

"This is the last Christmas at Our Lady of Peace." She sniffs.

A stunned silence covers us. I have no fond

memories of the place. The school was crowded, the teachers never the most supportive. I had so many demerits that they had a special chair for me in the principal's office. Masses were long and dull. The priests' sermons never taught me anything about the real world. But I grew up there as much as I grew up in my own house.

It was where I learned about friends, and girls, and how to navigate in the world. And how to pray, even if I don't do that much nowadays. And it was Momma's refuge. Now more than ever she probably needs that familiarity as Pop becomes more of a stranger.

And it will be gone. Sold to someone who will probably turn it into a restaurant or performance art theater.

"You'll like Saint John's," Maria assures her, breaking the quiet.

And with that, we finish preparing for the snowy walk.

We step outside, and a few of the little kids jump ahead and stomp through the accumulated snow. But most of us pause and look to the clear sky, dotted with stars and flakes. This moment is more precious than anything that will be said at mass.

This is the moment I realize I will always have my family, and I will find room for them in my life. A life with Gina, my career, and the Rinaldis. That's pretty much all I need.

GINA

I bounce down the steps and flop onto the couch. I've finished wrapping the gifts and have enough time to make something nice for breakfast.

Noises come from the kitchen.

"Nonna? You're awake already?" I spring up and follow the sounds.

"I can't have someone come for Christmas breakfast and not have food ready." Nonna fusses about. There's ham, biscuits, fruit, and the cheeses and meats present at every Italian meal.

"I was going to do all that." I swipe a piece of cheese and get my hand smacked.

"You make sure the living room is tidy."

"It is."

She raises an eyebrow.

"I was just there." I cringe. "Okay. I'll go look."

Nonna follows me, carrying a platter. "Do you think I made enough?"

"Chris is one person. We'll have to bring the rest to Aunt Sophia's house."

"Is he coming with us there?" Nonna's voice is controlled, but I sense the anxiety underneath.

"Can he?" I so want Chris to spend the day with us. Not only because I want to be with him. My cousins, my family can see that I have a boyfriend. Something they never expected me to have.

"Who am I to say no?"

"Thank you." I fling my arms around her. She's tiny, has always been tiny. But I think she's been shrinking. "Do you want your gift now?"

"I have food in the kitchen." Nonna bustles back. It was enough for her to allow Chris to spend the entire day with us. She's going to have to endure her sister's dirty looks all afternoon.

The doorbell chimes, and I yank open the door. Chris is bundled against the cold. It snowed last night, and now the streets are iced over.

"Merry Christmas." He steps in and kisses me. A chaste peck, because we're in Nonna's house, but he whispers, "I have mistletoe back at my place. Can you come home with me later?"

"I have mistletoe designs printed on my panties," I whisper back. "Maybe you can see them tonight."

He groans, but straightens himself when Nonna enters with two more platters.

"Merry Christmas, Mrs. Abate."

"*Buon Natale*. Gina says you'll be spending the day with us."

"If that's okay. I have a panna cotta for your sister." He holds out a gift bag from a gourmet shop.

Nonna nods approval. "Set it down. We'll bring it with us."

"Can we please exchange gifts now?" I bob on the balls of my feet.

Nonna smiles. "You always loved Christmas morning." She shuffles to the closet to extract some packages.

"You first, then." Chris hands me a giant, flat box from a department store with a giant red ribbon.

I pull open the ribbon and lift off the lid. A startling white coat nestles in tissue paper. It's just like the one I admired as we walked along Fifth Avenue.

"Chris, it's beautiful." I hug and kiss him. A real kiss on the lips, and I don't care that Nonna is watching. I stand to put it on. "This is the warmest thing I have ever worn. Thanks."

"The white makes your hair stand out good," Nonna approves.

"You're gorgeous."

Nonna fidgets with a small box on her lap. "I have a little something." She offers it.

Nonna will never have the money for the kind of gift Chris gets me, but I'm eager to see inside. Bubble wrap encases an ornament. It's a ceramic angel topper, accented with gold paint.

I hold it up, turning it around. "Thank you. It's beautiful."

Nonna's voice is soft. "Every woman in my family gets an angel when they reach adulthood and get their own house and their own tree." She flutters her hands in her lap. "I thought it was time. I didn't want to miss the chance to give it to you."

Tears pour over my face. I rush to her side and kneel in front of her chair. "Nonna, I'll always be here for you." I lay my head on her lap, and she strokes my hair.

"Gina *mia*, I know you will. But soon, you'll have your own place, as you should."

Chris clears his throat and rubs his face. I don't want to look too much, because he probably doesn't want to be caught crying.

"And this is one for you, Chris." Nonna produces a flat square wrapped in shiny paper.

"Thank you." Chris makes sure not to rip the paper. He must have an Italian grandmother as well, who saves every scrap. "A CD of Italian opera."

"I heard you singing to Gina. You have a good voice. You should sing more."

"I will. I'll sing to Gina every day."

Nonna purses her lips.

"And this is for you." I hand Chris a velvet box.

His brows knit in confusion. When he opens it, his eyes widen.

"It was my father's watch. I had the jeweler fix it up. A new band, new crystal, and got it running again."

"Gina." He exhales. "It's amazing."

"You don't wear one. But at that work party we went to, all the men wore expensive-looking watches. You need one to fit in. Not sure if this one is as fancy as the others."

"It's perfect." He straps it on his wrist, and I admire his hands.

It's Christmas, and I shouldn't be having these thoughts, but I want him.

"Looks good on you." Nonna cuts through my fantasy.

"Nonna. I didn't forget you." I present her with her favorite bath salts and lotion, the expensive kind that she never buys for herself.

She smiles broadly and kisses the top of my head.

"This is for you, Mrs. Abate." Chris hands her a tall box.

She eyes it, then unwraps it carefully. "Sambuca." Her voice rises. She taps the box with her finger. "This, this is a gift."

"I'm glad you like it, Mrs. Abate."

"Call me Nonna. Everyone does."

No one calls her Nonna but me, and I have to consciously close my mouth.

"I'll make coffee to go with this."

"Nonna, we haven't even eaten yet."

"So? It's Christmas." She shuffles into the kitchen.

"Guess that worked better than the flowers and cookies," Chris whispers.

I let go of the laugh that's been building in me.

"Do you want to take your coat off? It's warm in here."

"I want to take everything off." I kiss his ear and run my hand through his hair.

"Behave. I have to get through an entire afternoon with your family."

"Nonna's coming around." I look toward the kitchen.

"It's my charm."

I punch his arm. "I've got to finish getting dressed. I'll be right back. Don't annoy Nonna."

"Don't worry. Just come down soon. I only bought one bottle of sambuca."

GINA

The music carries down the hall, and as we approach Franny and Zack's apartment, Chris squeezes my hand.

"Nervous?" I ask.

"I want them to like me. I'm not sure I'll fit in with your friends."

I lean my head against his shoulder. "That's my line."

My knock isn't heard, but the door is ajar, so I push it open. The middle of the room is bare of furniture and filled with about twenty people from design school.

We halt inside the doorway and Zack appears with two plastic cups.

"Happy New Year!" He offers the cups of punch

225

to us.

"Hi, Zack. This is Chris."

Chris takes a cup and shakes Zack's hand. "Nice to meet you."

"It's nice to meet *you*. You're Gina's only distraction from her studies." Zack smiles and holds out the cup to me.

I hesitate.

"I'll hold Gina's," Chris offers.

"No, it's okay." I take a deep breath. "Zack, I don't drink."

"Okay." He shrugs and drinks from the cup himself. "There's sodas in the fridge. Help yourself. I've got to check on the playlist. I think Franny queued up that emo crap she listens to. Gina, you know everyone—introduce your guy around."

The tightness in my chest eases. Chris's eyes are wide.

"That was easy," I say. "Maybe that should be my line all the time."

"Yeah. But I can't imagine the crowd at a Humbolt and Sutter party not raising an eyebrow. They'd probably assume you're a recovering alcoholic." He takes a sip and grimaces. "You're not missing anything. This punch is half sugar, half moonshine, and half red coloring."

"Would that be a problem? Everyone at your work thinking I'm an alcoholic?" I slip out of my coat and drop it on the pile of others. Then hold the offending punch so Chris can do the same.

"The only thing people think about when they see us together is why a stunning girl like you is with a guy like me."

I hit him on the arm. "Not true." But it's nice to hear.

We join the crowd, and Chris's charming personality shines. He could fit in anywhere, even with the design people. His humble background, the one-percenters he moves with now, and everyone in between. Chris puts people at ease, and I admire him for that. I might have made enormous gains and can mix in any social situation, but I'll never be the life of the party. I'll never be the center of attention, at least not in a good way.

"You're Chris." Franny bounces over.

"You have a great place." Chris raises his cup to her. "Nice party. Thanks for having me."

"Are you kidding? We've all been dying to meet you. Gina's Wall Street dude."

"I hope I live down to those expectations." Chris pulls me to him.

Franny's eyes mist over. "I'm glad you're as kind as Gina says."

We drink and talk. We try dancing in Franny's tiny bedroom. I find myself laughing and palling around the way people with friends do.

I can recall a party at my cousin's house. It was her fourteenth birthday, and I guess her mother made her invite me, since we were the same age. A crowd of kids stood around just like this. Only then, I pressed my back against the wall of the living room, praying the music would get softer, the voices would stop talking so loudly, and the disco ball would stop spinning and giving off its flashes of light.

But now it's easy. Even the loud countdown to the New Year doesn't irritate my eardrums.

When the ball drops on television, and we all scream "Happy New Year," Chris grabs my waist and pulls me against him. His back is pressed to the wall, and I straddle one of his legs. Our mouths connect and the world fades away. I'm able to block everything else out. For the first time in my life, I focus on just this one sensation.

Really, the many sensations. His hands grip my butt, his tongue sweeps my mouth, and his breath feathers my skin.

He pulls back, and I'm lost in his eyes. "Happy New Year." My voice is raspy with desire of more than just a kiss.

"And many more, sweetheart." He brings me in for another kiss.

Many more. I flash back to the jewelry box. *Please don't ask me to marry you now. I just became the person I am.* And yet another part wants nothing else but to spend every minute of my new life with him.

"Quit making out. It's a party," Zack calls.

But the party soon breaks up. People have

coupled up and seem intent on finding more private places.

"We should help clean up," Chris says as he glances around the wreck of the apartment.

"And then back to your place?" I singsong.

"Baby, you don't know how fast I can gather empty cups."

He gets to work on the table, and I pick up the streamers from the floor.

"Thanks for helping," Franny says as she brings out a big trash bag.

"No problem." I stuff a bunch of paper plates in the bag she holds open. "This was the best party I've ever been to. I can't tell you how happy I am." I hug Franny, and the trash bag is smushed between us.

"Okay." There's a question in her voice. "Did you have too much to drink?"

"Gina doesn't drink," Zack adds from the kitchen.

"Just high on life, huh?" Franny bends down to retrieve a plate that found its way under her couch.

"There's something I should tell you two."

Chris freezes in what he is doing. His face contorts into fear. Fear that I'll embarrass him or myself, I don't know. But Franny and Zack are real friends.

"You're not pregnant, are you?" Franny eyes me. "Is that why you're not drinking? You'd better take care of her." She turns on Chris, who holds up his hands in surrender.

"No. I'm not pregnant." I take a deep breath. "Chris, it's okay. I want to tell them. I'm taking medication, which is why I can't drink. It's because I have autism."

"That's it?" Zack turns from me to Chris. "That's the big build-up? I was hoping for something juicier."

"Really?" Franny wrinkles her forehead. "My cousin's autistic, and you don't seem like him at all."

"There are many different ways autism manifests itself," Chris pipes in. "Sorry, you go ahead."

"Chris has done a lot of research on autism since we've been together."

He blushes and returns to cleaning up.

"But he's right. And up until a few months ago I wouldn't have been able to come to a party like this. I never felt normal until my new treatment."

Zack laughs. "Gina, maybe the only reason you finally feel normal is because you have me and Franny as friends now."

"He's right. Did you take a good look at the other students? Not a normal one in the bunch," Franny adds.

Chris's face relaxes into a sad grin. He nods and gives me a thumbs-up.

He's relieved, at peace that he doesn't have to bear the burden of knowing my secret alone. I can tell others now. Maybe not the Humbolt and Sutter people, but my people.

Zack and Franny have gone back to cleaning, and my autism doesn't matter. It doesn't matter because of the miracle drug and because I'm a new me.

Chapter 20

This will be the big test. Sunday dinner. The Rinaldis versus the Giancarlos.

Gina and her grandmother are coming over after church. Gina couldn't convince her grandmother to come to Our Lady of Peace. So we each sat through services at our respective churches.

The January chill bites at our faces as we walk back to the house.

"Your balls grow to elephant size since you've been in the city?" Marco falls into step with me.

"My pants wouldn't fit." I brace myself against a blast of wind and whatever Marco is going to hurl at me.

"Inviting Regina and her grandmother for Sunday dinner." Marco laughs. "What did Momma say?"

"I politely asked her if they could come, and she agreed." I hunch into my coat. "If you all want to be in my life, you might have to be in hers as well."

"That bad, huh?" He shakes his head and

hurries to the front door.

Momma has already shed her coat and is thumping pots around in the kitchen.

"Momma, let me help." I pull an apron off a hook and tie it around me.

She raises an eyebrow then lifts a shoulder. "You were the only one of my sons who ever learned to cook." She points to a cutting board.

I chop bell peppers and search for what I want to say. Talking to my mother was never easy. Besides the fact that she's not a heart-to-heart kind of person, she was usually too busy running a large family for any extended conversation.

"Thanks for having Gina and her grandmother today."

"Was I going to say no? And let them think I wouldn't have them in my home?" She waves a sauce-covered spoon. "No. If they can admit that Gina was wrong and come here to apologize, it's the least I can do to accept their apology. It's up to God to forgive them."

"Momma, they're not coming to apologize, they're coming for dinner." Sweat beads on my brow, and not from the oven heating up.

"When is your girlfriend getting here?" Maria enters the kitchen and walks over to me.

"I sent a car for them at Saint John's. They should be here in a few minutes."

"You sent a car? What, are you a garage now?"

233

She snatches a pepper from the board I'm working on and crunches it between her teeth, which are overshadowed by her fire-engine-red lips.

"It's a long trip, especially in the cold."

"And what's going to happen when we have to make the same trip when they close Our Lady? Hmm?" Momma says.

I finish the last pepper, elbow Maria out of the way, and scrape them into the pan Momma is working with. Some of the pieces miss the pan and scatter to the floor.

Momma doesn't flinch. In fact, she becomes as still as a cheetah stalking prey about to pounce.

"Some spilled." Her voice is dead calm.

"I'll clean it up. It was my fault." Maria bends down.

"No, I'll get it. Momma and I have some things to discuss."

Maria raises her eyebrow higher but leaves.

I dump the peppers in the trash and square my shoulders.

"I've explained it all to you. Gina and I read the report. We—"

"Shush." The cheetah has uncoiled and latched its jaws on the soft throat of the gazelle.

I'm the gazelle.

"I don't want to hear another word about that." She continues, "All that matters is what you told me. You said they wanted to make amends. You called me on the phone from your big, important, high-finance job to say that your girlfriend and her nonna want to come to dinner. You want them to come here so we can all get along and put the past behind us. You said that. You said they were sorry."

"I said they were sorry about how they let the friction get out of hand. Gina is sorry that things didn't go well the last time she was here. But she has nothing to be sorry about in regards to Carina's death."

"That's not what I think." Momma coolly returns to her work.

"That's not what—" I stop myself, realizing I am yelling. Momma hears what she wants to hear.

My voice has summoned most of my siblings and their spouses. A sea of Rinaldi faces crowd the doorway to the kitchen.

"This is supposed to be a private conversation," I say very slowly.

This brings out a few laughs, but no one moves to leave.

I face Momma again. "All I can tell you for sure is that I love Gina. She is going to be in my life, maybe forever. So if you want me in your life, you'd better figure out a way to make peace."

Momma places her hands on her hips and readies for another attack.

"Chris, your guests are here," Donny calls from the living room.

Whatever Momma was going to say will be lost forever. Mustering my best warning glower toward Momma, I paste on a charming grin and greet Gina and her grandmother.

"Hi, Chris." Gina's smile is as strained as mine. She pecks me on the cheek, and I help her and her nonna out of their coats.

"Come in, say hi to everyone."

Marco at least makes an effort and takes her nonna's hand to lead her to the couch. "You must be frozen, Mrs. Abate. Can I get you some coffee?"

"Thank you, that's very kind." Nonna perches on the couch, and Gina joins her.

Silence never lasts long in the Rinaldi house, and a few kids scamper through, eliciting warnings from some of the adults, and the babble of conversations picks up.

Momma emerges from the kitchen with a delicate rose-patterned china cup filled with steaming coffee. It's one of the cups from the set of china I have yet to eat off. I've seen Father McCurdy eat off those plates, and I've seen the local councilman drink from those cups. But I've never even touched one.

"Mrs. Abate, I heard you wanted something to warm you up from that long trip from Saint John's."

Momma offers the cup, and Nonna accepts. We all stare at this peace offering.

Gina is holding her breath. Nonna's precise

movements entrance us as she lifts the cup to her lips.

Her eyes widen and she licks her upper lip. "That sure does warm the soul." She beams.

"Christofo told me you liked sambuca." Momma nods and bustles back to the kitchen. "Dinner will be out in a moment," she calls. "Christofo, make sure our guests have everything they need."

Gina giggles, and I can't control the nervous laughter escaping from me either.

Marco slaps my back. "Momma's sharing her sambuca. I wouldn't be surprised if the United Nations announced world peace."

The conversation soon turns to the neighborhood gossip and which of the Battaglia kids got arrested last time, and when are they ever going to fix the potholes.

Momma announces dinner and holds a chair out for Gina's nonna at her right side.

"Mrs. Abate, sit with me."

"Thank you, Mrs. Rinaldi." She scoots her chair in and smiles naturally. I didn't realize she was capable of that level of warmth and sincerity.

"Call me Rose," Momma says.

"And you call me Catherine."

"I didn't know your name was Catherine," I blurt out.

"Why would you?" Gina's nonna says, and turns her attention to Momma.

Grace is run through fairly quickly.

The two are thick as thieves the rest of the meal. Rehashing stories from decades ago, commiserating over family illnesses.

Gina barely eats anything. Her mouth hangs open in disbelief most of the time.

"I'm sorry my husband can't join us." Momma dabs at her mouth.

"Think nothing of it." Mrs. Abate waves away the remark. "Life is not easy. Full of challenges."

"And these kids don't understand that. They think everything will always work out in the end."

Mrs. Abate nods slowly. "They rush into everything." She glances at me.

Momma joins in the glare-at-Chris activity. "I was just telling my son, not everything works out as you think it's going to. It takes time."

"Wise words, Rose." Mrs. Abate raises her cup in a salute.

Momma returns it.

Message received. Don't propose to Gina…yet.

GINA

The door to the Autism Center flings open and is pinned against the wall by the wind.

Nonna squeals, and I help her step inside and yank the door closed behind us.

"Oh." Nonna unwraps the scarf from her face

and I pull off my mittens. February has become bitter, the glow of the holidays behind us.

But today is special. Jennifer has asked Nonna to come with me because the study is over. I've given my last blood sample and taken my last personality and cognitive tests.

From now on I can take the medication on a regular basis without all the oversight.

"Do you think I'll still have to come here?" I ask Nonna as we wait for the elevator.

"Why would you stop? You like Jennifer."

"I like her fine. But I don't need to see her anymore, do I?" I bounce on the balls of my feet and spring into the elevator.

Nonna follows and glares at me to settle down. I do, because no matter how much I have grown in the past few months, she's still my nonna.

The receptionist waves us through and Jennifer sits in her desk chair staring at the wall. Her brow is furrowed and she fiddles with a paper clip.

"Jennifer?"

"Gina, Mrs. Abate, come in." She stands and shuts the door behind us.

We sit on Jennifer's threadbare couch. I've wanted to make a slipcover for it for years.

"I want to get straight to the point of the meeting. Because this ending is not an easy thing to discuss."

"See, Nonna. I told you. Jennifer, I'll come back

to visit. There's no way I can say good-bye forever."

"Gina." Jennifer holds up a hand. "It can't come as a surprise to you that you were the only person to benefit from the medication."

"I know. I feel terrible for Jerome and the others—"

"Gina." Jennifer meets my gaze. "The study is over. The company, Genloran, isn't going to be producing the drug. They're halting any further studies."

"Do you mean I was the only, only one to get better? Ever?"

Nonna's hand covers mine. Her fingers are warm but bony.

"Yes, that's what I mean." Jennifer swallows. "They won't be producing the medication."

I steady my breathing. "When you say they won't be producing it, you mean making it for everyone. I can still buy it somewhere, right?"

She shakes her head and clears her throat. She opens her mouth, but closes it again. Her eyes fill with tears.

"No." I shake my head. "No."

Nonna tries to pull me to her, but I break away and shoot up.

"They can't do that. They can't make me better then expect me to go back. Go back to—to... Oh God." I sink to the floor.

I don't care if the racking sobs echo off the walls

and alert everyone in the building.

"No," I wail over and over.

They need to hear my anguish. They need to know what they've done to me.

Nonna and Jennifer crouch on either side, and it's suffocating. I dash from the room and race down the hall to the nurse's office.

This is where I have come to pick up the pills. Every week for months, I took those pills. I swallowed the chalky circles. I endured the nausea. I went through the tests, the blood draws.

I pound on the closed door. My face is soaked with tears and snot.

"It's not fair." I scream until my throat is hoarse.

I slide down the wall and end up sprawled on the floor. Not much registers as the nurse appears and helps Jennifer bring me into her office. There's murmuring and fussing. I'm handed a glass of water that I want to smash on the floor, but find the control to take a gentle sip.

The water soothes the harshness in my throat but doesn't do a thing for my pounding head.

Nonna and Jennifer leave, and I'm alone with Gloria, the nurse.

"Take some more water," she encourages me.

I do, but only because there's no use in fighting anything or anyone. Soon I'll go back to the agreeable and distant person I was for the first twenty-four years of my life. If I wanted, I could probably figure out how many months and days as well. But I don't want to. That will come back.

"Why?" I ask.

"Who knows? There are some things science doesn't explain. It's possible that you had a spontaneous recovery. That's what they're calling it, anyway." She crosses to her locked medication cabinet. "It could be the placebo effect. You've been learning about emotions and social skills for years. Maybe you took to them because you believed you would." She pulls out a large white bottle and drags a chair to sit next to me.

"I got your grandmother and Jennifer to leave us alone for a few minutes." She places the bottle in front of me on the table. "It's not just my job, but my license to practice nursing, that I might lose."

I shake my head. "Huh?"

"It's what's left of the drug. I'm supposed to return it all to Genloran. I'll give them a few tablets, but you keep the rest."

"How much longer?"

"Try cutting the pills in half to see if that dose is enough." She sighs. "Like I said, it could be postponing the inevitable, or maybe you never needed the drug after all. These could be placebos. It's a double blind study. I have no idea if these are the real ones or not."

With my index finger, I caress the cap.

"Should I tell people that I might change back?"

I hiccough. "There are some people who I met recently who won't even know what to expect."

"At this point I would talk to the people you love. You'll need their support." She pushes the bottle toward me and I drop it into my purse.

"There's only one person I need to warn."

Chapter 21

CHRIS

I'm finally going to pull the trigger.

Gina's settled at school. I'm cruising along, one of Breckner's favorites. There's no reason we shouldn't get married now.

Despite the fierce wind, I feel my face split into a grin. The normal two-block walk from the subway to my apartment seems so much longer because of the weather, but mostly because Gina's coming over.

If Gina and I were married, she could live in my apartment. I'd take care of all the finances until she started working. She'd build a career for herself. She could work part-time when the babies came.

I've never thought about fatherhood before. And after Carina died, I figured I didn't deserve to be a father.

But watching Pop deteriorate makes me realize how much he meant to me, how important he was in my life, and how I could be the same to a little Chris. Or a little Gina.

I practically jog the rest of the way to my front door.

"That babe is waiting in the lobby for you." Jack, my nosy doorman, elbows me in the ribs. "She's been pacing around, checking the time. Don't waste a second getting upstairs. She's hot for it now."

"Is this the kind of training you get at doorman school?" I sneer at him and enter.

Gina is biting her fingernails and leaps when I come in.

"You okay?" I dart to her and hold her shoulders.

"Let's go upstairs." She hurries to the elevator, but Jack's wrong. She's not anxious to get upstairs to tear off our clothes.

On the ride up, she chews her lip and refuses to look at me. I take a deep breath. There's no point in asking her anything until we get inside, but my heart rate is increasing, and not in a good way.

My hand shakes as I unlock the door. I haven't seen Gina this upset since we opened the file on Carina's death.

"You want something to drink?" I ask, not sure if I want her to say yes to postpone whatever is coming, or if I want her to say no and get to the bottom of this.

"They stopped making my medication." She perches on the edge of the couch and wrings her hands.

"What do you mean?" I join her and reach to hold her hands, but she jerks away, turning her body at an angle.

"The study is over. I'm the only one who had any benefit. If I did have any benefit." She holds the sides of her head and presses.

"What? Of course you benefitted. That drug was a huge success."

"Why? Because one measly girl from Queens seemed to have been cured? That's not how it works. Those companies don't care about people. They don't care." Her voice breaks with an anguished moan.

"I meant — I only meant so what if the trial was a failure? You're a success."

"So? How does that help me now? This is all I have left." She pulls a large white bottle from her purse. Pills rattle inside. "And they might only be placebos."

"I'm sure we can find someone to make it. I'll pay whatever it costs." I caress her back, but she flinches.

"No can do. No amount of your money can fix this. Genloran has a patent on the formula, and so no one else can make and sell it." She turns now, and her wild, red-rimmed eyes bore into me. "What's it going to be? You want an autistic girlfriend who can never get a joke, can never hold a normal conversation, can never — " She gulps for air.

"Gina, it won't be like that." I try to pull her to me.

"And what if it is?" She keeps her distance,

waiting for my answer.

"I'll stick with you. It will be okay."

"Like you stuck around after Carina died?"

My vision blurs and there's a clanging in my ears. I shake my head and bolt from the couch. "You didn't just say that." My voice is barely above a whisper.

"Maybe I didn't mean that. Maybe I did. You see? Even now I can't tell what's right or wrong to say." She laughs bitterly. "And even if you did stay with me, then what? You'd be resentful. I would have stolen from you the life you wanted. The life you've worked so hard for." She exhales, puts the pills away, and stands. "It's best if we don't see each other. At least until I can find out what's going to happen to me."

"Gina, don't. Don't do this. I need you. I want you."

"You want the Gina I am now. Would you have wanted me before?" She holds up her hand. "Honestly, Chris. You knew me back then. Did you ever think about me the way you think about me now?"

"That's different. I was a different person, too." My lungs constrict. This can't be happening. I've never had a woman walk out on me before. It's worse than I thought it would feel. Because it's a woman I actually care about.

"I'll call you later." She strides to the door.

"Don't call me until I figure things out."

I stand but don't follow. What's the point? She's gone, and the only bulge in my pants is from the velvet jewelry box.

GINA

Nonna turns the chicken in the pan, and the usually comforting scent of lemon and capers wafts to me at the table.

She has given up trying to engage me in conversation. Since I got back from Chris's place, I've shut her out. I can't bring myself to talk anymore to anyone.

A plate of chicken piccata, roasted potatoes, and string beans appears before me. My favorite meal.

"Thanks," I croak.

Nonna's worried smile brings back the memory of when I had my appendix out. Back then I couldn't parse the difference between the happy grin on her mouth and the anxious slant of her eyes. But now I get it.

My knife makes measured cuts of the meat. The first forkful is like mud in my mouth. Methodical chews make it possible to swallow. I clatter my fork down.

"Sorry," I mutter.

"It's okay." Nonna swipes the plate away and packs the food in plastic containers.

The file cabinet is just out of reach from my chair. I scoot over and pull out the papers that vacated my conservatorship.

I place them in the center of Nonna's sparkling clean table—the few pages stapled at the corner.

Tearing it up now won't mean Nonna's my conservator again, but it's something we need to think about.

"Gina mia, don't think like that." She sits next to me and places her hand on mine. "Maybe you will stay the way you are now."

"And maybe I won't. I think we should go back to court."

"I can't." Her weary tone lets me know she's as exhausted as I am. "I'm almost seventy. I won't be here forever. Besides, even if you do..." She waves her hand. "You're going to have your degree and a career. You can take care of yourself."

"Mostly." I finger the sharp end of the staple that sticks out a bit. "If I'm able to finish school."

"If you're worried, maybe you should ask Christopher to be the conservator." Nonna averts her gaze from me.

I'm not sure why a laugh bubbles up. "*Now* you like him."

"He's shown himself to be a good man. And he's smart about money."

"I'm smart about money." I scrape the chair as I stand. "I don't think I should date Chris anymore."

"Now *you* don't like him," she huffs.

"I like him too much to condemn him to a life with me."

"Nonsense. If he loves you, then he loves you."

"It's not simple like that. He has a life that requires him to be charming and go to parties and wine and dine people. He can't have someone like me on his arm screwing it all up."

"Anyone would be lucky to have —"

"Why did Momma have the small room down here when all the older kids had bedrooms upstairs?"

"Why are you asking me that now?" Nonna fusses with the pan, which is already clean, but she's found a spot to scrub.

"Was Momma autistic?"

"No." Her back is to me as she stands at the sink, but her shoulders fall, and I know she's wearing that sad expression she gets whenever she thinks of my mother. "I didn't expect one more. Thought I was too old for another baby. But Theresa came along and we were happy to have her."

"Was Nonno Vic happy?"

"Why wouldn't he be?"

"Why was Momma downstairs by herself when all her siblings had rooms upstairs?"

"Because she was special to me." Nonna turns, her face streaked with wet tracks of tears. "I treasured her, pampered her, spoiled her. And she attached herself to that no-good louse who abandoned you two when—" She clamps her mouth shut.

"When they figured out I would never develop like other kids." I nod. "I don't expect Chris is much different than other men in that way." I fold the corner of the conservatorship papers. "I thought Momma had to stay downstairs because she was the wild one."

"The other way around." Nonna sinks into the seat.

"Not your fault. I think we're all meant to be a certain way. We're all born with capacities and personalities, and nothing can change that. Not even magic pills. I'm sorry I'm not hungry. I'll eat later. I'm going to lie down."

I flop on my bed and squeeze my eyes shut. But open them right away. The last thing I want to do is focus on my thoughts. They might stray to strings of prime numbers. But I don't want to focus on the world either. Certainly not the incessant texts that keep pinging on my phone.

I look. Five from Chris and two from Jennifer.

I do the only thing I know I still can do—rearrange my furniture. I pull the drawers out of the dresser so it's easier to move. I've always wanted to try my bed on the other side of the room, and the classic rock station is the perfect accompaniment. The volume of the speakers won't go louder, but still the texts light my phone up.

Fine, I'll answer Jennifer. She's probably worried about me.

I scroll through Chris's texts quickly. I don't want to see his sympathy and concern. Because he is as concerned for himself and the relationship he is losing as he is for me.

Instead of reading Jennifer's, I call.

"Gina, I'm so glad you called. How are you doing?"

"Shitty, shitty, shitty." I take a deep breath. "Unless you're calling to tell me they're going to keep giving me the medicine, I'm not sure there's anything I can say."

"You need to believe in yourself, Gina. You made this progress. Maybe the drug helped. The drug might have made it possible. But you were the one brave enough to try, and to learn."

"You mean stupid enough. Jennifer, I like you. You've been there for me and my grandmother for years. I know you want to see me succeed. But let's face it, no one gets cured from autism."

"Did you think this was a cure?" Her tone is that scolding one she uses when someone has been inappropriate in group.

"Didn't you?" I scold right back.

Her silence shows her shame.

My side table is in the center of the room, my desk lamp on the floor, and the mattress is on the side.

"I've been autistic once. I'll be autistic again." I walk to my chair and stub my toe on the edge of the dresser. "Shit." Tears spring to my eyes. "I thought I was done crying."

"Gina, maybe you've been autistic this entire time." Jennifer's voice has become soft again.

"If that's true, then they better come up with a better definition of autism."

Chapter 22

CHRIS

I don't even care that the coffee is black and bitter.

I'll never drink another mochaccino again. Even if they are cheaper at the new coffee shop I go to. I tried calling Gina another three times last night before I flung my phone across the room.

When it shattered against the television, I didn't flinch. What was buying another phone and a new TV when I had nothing else?

I stare at my monitor. There are a gazillion emails, and I mindlessly click through them.

Idiosyncratic Drug-Induced Liver Injury catches my eye.

"Of course," I mutter as I read the message from one of my pharma contacts. I guess it's a good thing that Genloran is pulling all of the meds back. Turns out four of the people in the study had liver problems. A cold cramp wrenches my gut where I think my liver sits. What if Gina's liver is affected? Nothing would be worth that. Will she feel the same? Will she risk her health for the changes in her life?

Maybe in a few days she'll see that it doesn't

matter about the medicine. Maybe all the gains she made will stick without it. Maybe she got better on her own and took the placebo. Her liver blood tests must have been normal or they would have said something.

My email pings a priority message from Breckner. He wants me in his office now.

A premonition of what this is about chews on the back of my brain. And if I ever get my hands on that good-for-nothing ex-frat brother of mine...

I stalk down the hall, not acknowledging the greetings from the traders.

I step into Breckner's office and take the chair he wordlessly indicates with a wave of his hand. My gut sinks even lower than my ass does in the plush leather.

"I'm sure you know already," he says.

"Genloran stopped production of their drug. Looks like the clinical trials weren't all that successful. In fact, some people might have had adverse effects."

"That's an understatement." He pulls up a new window on his screen. "Genloran reports projected earnings to drop fifteen percent this quarter. You weren't the only one putting all your eggs in one basket."

"Guess not, sir." I shuffle my feet. "There's no point in trying to make excuses. I laid it on red and it came up black. I'll take my lumps."

"Good to see you're manning up." Breckner stood and paced slowly to the window, the double window, the corner window. The window I will probably never get at this point. "You're a smart man, Rinaldi. You know which way the wind blows. You know how to communicate with the traders, as well as the board. I suspect you've scrabbled up from Staten Island to your Midtown condo."

"Queens."

"Same thing." He turns to face me. "The good news is that this sort of thing happens all the time, and we've covered our bases. Our investors expect ups and downs."

"Thanks."

"The bad news is that whenever we do have a significant loss, we do a small internal investigation. Just to see where we went wrong and how to prevent it again. We never do prevent the occasional loss. There's no way to do that. But it shows we take it seriously when we lose our investors' money."

"I do take it seriously. I don't want you to think I was some kind of cowboy riding in to take over the town."

Breckner smirks. "Yes, you were. But that's okay. Just a good thing you didn't have any inside information about the drug. Correct?"

My mouth goes dry, my throat closes, and my lungs can't seem to get air.

"Chris?"

"My expert was never employed by Genloran. He worked in pharma but never at that company."

"Good, then there's nothing to worry about."

Except the fact that I am dating the only patient to benefit from the drug. And maybe we aren't even dating anymore.

"You can go now. I'll let you know if we need anything for the investigation."

"Thanks, Bob." I stand. "Guess my first big move flopped, huh?"

"You're not the only one. You're smart enough to learn from your mistakes."

I trudge back to my office.

Still no word from Gina.

My desperation to talk to her ratchets up a few notches. Now I have to convince her to get back together with me while at the same time convince her to lie about ever having told me anything about the drug.

Even I'm not that charming.

GINA

I take the chalky tablet and position it on the square of waxed paper. I lower the knife down the middle of it slowly, but still I need to apply enough force to split it apart. A flinder escapes and flies to the edge of the waxed paper. Tears spring to my eyes, but I can't do anything about it now. I must save every milligram. My career, my happiness, and my personality rest in these grains.

Carefully, I tip the end of the paper up. Powder collects in the fold.

I'll take the smaller half today along with the powder and fragments. The full half will be easier to save for later.

I sprinkle it to the back of my throat and pray that it's absorbed into my bloodstream.

Nonna is watching me from the doorway.

"Gina mia, it will be okay. We'll find something else."

"There is nothing else, Nonna." The anger in my voice doesn't surprise me or her. But it might be one of the last times we hear it. I treasure that anger, want to hold it, want it to linger between us. A real emotion born of fright.

"Chris sent flowers." She points downstairs.

"Bring them to church." I squeeze past her and want nothing more than to shut myself in my room.

"You have work today." She trails behind me.

"I'll call in sick." I begin to shut my door.

"No, you won't." She places her solid body in the way, hands on hips, full Italian grandmother mode. "You'll go into work and do your job. Earn money and then go to your classes. If you're going to cut those pills into tiny bits, then you're going to fight for everything else. Don't give up on yourself, Gina *mia*. No one else has."

The sobs tumble out. I crumple into her arms and allow the sadness to envelop me.

When I first started to feel these emotions, I hated the sad ones. I only wanted the good ones. Now, I know I'll miss them both. I'll take desperation, anxiety, and grief over nothing any day.

GINA

The subway stops in a tunnel. While we wait for the train in front of us to move, we stare ahead, not seeing the people around us. You're not supposed to make eye contact or smile. Or search a stranger's face for clues about their emotional state. Each person exists in their own private world. To get by in New York City, everyone needs to be a little autistic.

The few blocks to the coffee shop blur past. I don't even try to look at people's faces.

I greet Sarah and Becky with a nod and a grunt and put my things away.

Chris doesn't come in for his order. He texted me and called me. I haven't responded.

Like a machine, I plod through the morning.

"Okay, Gina. What gives?" Becky harumphs when the last morning customer leaves.

"They're not making my medication anymore. I have about fifteen pills left."

"What are you talking about?" Sarah asks.

"The changes I've made. The improvements. It's

because I've been taking an experimental drug."

"It can't all be from a drug," Sarah says. "I mean, you were learning things the entire time, still going to the Autism Center, taking classes at Reynolds—"

"I knew something was up." Becky snaps her fingers.

"Becky, clean out the back room," Sarah orders. "And the bathroom."

Becky clomps two steps away and then stops. "Gina, sorry about your medicine. You've been more fun to be around lately. I hope it all works out for you." She continues to the back room without looking back.

"I like her better when she's being a bitch." I scrub the counter. "Watching other people pity me." I shake my head. "That I can't handle. Hopefully, I'll be too far gone to realize it's happening."

"Are you sure that's going to happen? I mean, maybe you won't, you know, go back." Sarah's eyes dart away from me. She fiddles with the milk steamer, which doesn't need adjusting.

"I'll have to wait and see." My phone buzzes in my pocket for the millionth time.

"Are you going to get that?"

"It's Chris. I told him not to call me."

Sarah chuckles. "You did learn how to deal with men. Tell them not to call you and that's all they'll do until you answer." She counts the tea bags and restacks the boxes.

"Thanks for being a friend. Even before. I couldn't recognize how kind you were to me until… I want to tell you now…in case…."

"Shut up or I'll make you clean the bathroom with Becky."

I smile because Sarah needs to see that she's cheering me up, even if she isn't. Here's something I won't miss, having to respond with a certain emotion I don't feel so the other person feels better.

"You should at least go out with him to say good-bye." Sarah rinses the carafes a second time.

"Why? So he can try to convince me to stay together? So he can watch my descent back to the way I was?" I scrub the counter for the third time. If I don't keep moving, I'll think too much. I'll notice my abilities slip away.

"So they're really going to stop making your medicine? Just like that?"

"Just like that." I exhale and lean against the counter.

"It's not fair that they did this to you." Becky has returned. She keeps her distance by the pastry display. But her face is red, either from embarrassment or the effort it takes her to be civil. "You know, my sister works for the *Daily News,* and she would love to cover this story."

"I'm not sure what I'm allowed to say or not say."

"Are they allowed to yank the rug out from

under you like this?" Becky puts her hands on her hips.

"It might be good to call attention to what happened," Sarah adds.

Becky needs to redeem herself. I can see her guilt, it's an aura. She spent the first part of our relationship resenting me and being cruel. Then when I improved, she was jealous. Now, facing my deterioration, she faces her own failings.

"I'm not sure I want it splashed across the papers."

"Just meet with her." Becky inches forward, a cautious approach to atone.

"Sure," I agree. I've told everyone at school about my autism. So they'll all find out eventually when it reemerges from the depths of my brain.

Chapter 23

CHRIS

I fold and refold my napkin. Gina will walk through the restaurant door, she'll see me, I'll whip the napkin off the jewelry box, get down on one knee, and it will all be okay.

She finally agreed to meet me. A week once seemed like no time at all, but seven days without Gina is a lifetime.

There's no way she'll go back to the way she was. I know that in my heart. For so many years I didn't trust my heart, or even allow myself to acknowledge that I had one. Then Gina came along and made me rediscover passion, and not just the lusty kind. All because she discovered passion, too.

The door opens. Gina steps through. Her jeans conform to every curve, and the white down jacket I bought her for Christmas shows off her cascading auburn curls.

But her face shows the strain she's been under. Dark circles under her eyes and creases around her mouth erase the joy that was there just a few weeks ago when our families made amends.

She approaches, and I stand to pull out her chair.

I kiss her on the cheek and she returns the peck. Her dry lips perform an almost aggressive poke against my face.

"Thanks for meeting me." I take her hand and caress her palm.

"I don't know what there is to say."

"There's everything—" I wave the waiter carrying the sparkling apple juice away. Maybe in a few minutes, when she's lacing her ringed fingers around my neck and giving me one of her sensual kisses, we'll feel like celebrating. "Let's just talk, like we did before all this happened. Can't we try to have a dinner out?" I want her to remember all the fun times we had, the great conversations, the secrets we shared. "Tell me about school."

She huffs. "The spring semester started. Classes are interesting. I'm applying for internships at design companies." Her voice is flat, but I forge ahead.

"That's great. How are Zack and Franny?"

"Fine."

"How's your nonna?"

"As good as can be expected." She takes a sip of water and taps the menu. "I'm trying, Chris. Really I am." She looks at me and her emerald eyes are watery. She closes them and sits up straighter. "Tell me about your day. How is work going?"

"That might not be a topic to lighten the mood."

The waiter approaches to take our order. I wave him away a second time.

"What happened?" There's real concern in her face. At least I've distracted her from her problems.

"I feel terrible telling you this. It all happened before we started dating." I run my finger over my fork. "I told everyone to buy Genloran stock. I heard about the drug you were taking and recommended it. I didn't know you were taking it then. I didn't even know you."

She laughs, and soon her giggles become maniacal. I scan the dining room and a few heads turn our way, but maybe her laughter doesn't sound as disturbing as I think it does. She takes a deep breath and gains control. "We both got screwed by that company." Her crazy laughter is gone, but it's replaced with a fierce look of revenge.

"Neither of us is screwed. Money is no longer the most important thing in my life. And you are an amazing woman with or without the medication."

"I've thought about trying to find someone to make it for me. I'm out of pills."

"Good, don't take anymore. And let's hope you took the sugar pills. Four people had adverse reactions. You couldn't find someone to make them for you. No chemist or pharmacist would make something for you that might hurt you."

"But they'll make something to help me, and then yank it away."

"You don't need them. You need people who love you." I shift the napkin and reveal the box.

"Gina?"

I slide from my chair and get down on my knee. Her eyes go wide, and she freezes.

"I love you. I admire you. You've changed me to be a better man. I only want money so I can provide for you and our children." I open the box.

"Oh," she gasps, and touches the solitaire.

"I'll be there no matter what happens. I promise. If we can read the coroner's report from my sister's death, then we can get through this. I have faith in you. You can beat this. Say you'll be with me."

"I don't know." She starts to cry. "Please get off the floor. I can't think straight."

I return to my seat. But she hasn't said no, so I've still got a chance.

"Do...do you need to think about it? Can't you take the chance?"

"Not now. Maybe last week I could. My future is so uncertain. I've asked my grandmother to be my conservator again, but she says she's too old."

"You won't need someone to take care of you. And I can be there. Because of you, I've figured out my priorities for the first time since Carina died. The investigation at work doesn't even bother me if I know I've got you."

"What investigation?"

"It's routine when there's a major loss. They look for anything unethical or some reason I might have pushed Genloran stock. We're fine, just as long as no one knows your part in it." I take her hand and search her eyes for an answer, but she avoids my gaze.

"I'm going to speak out about what they did. It's not fair to me. There might be others in the country, or others in a different study. They can't give people hope and then douse it."

"What do you mean?" A knot forms in my gut.

"I've got an appointment to talk to a journalist. I might not agree to give a full interview, but I might. If I don't speak out for people who were wronged like I was, who will?"

"Gina, that will ruin me. Everyone at work knows we were together. You came to all the office parties. Your picture is still on my desk."

"I thought money doesn't matter to you anymore."

"It doesn't, except I still need a job. I sweated for that MBA. I can't throw it away because of a bad decision and a freak coincidence."

She reaches out, shuts the box, and pushes it toward me. "We need some time. I need to know if I'll lose everything I gained. I need to decide if I want to stand up for myself and others. You need to decide how to handle work. The last thing we need to do is plan a wedding."

I can't find any words as she slides her chair back and leaves. But I don't want to plan a wedding. I want to plan a life.

CHRIS

My hand shakes as I knock on Breckner's door.

"Come." The gruff voice vibrates through the heavy wooden door.

"Bob, you have a minute?"

"Chris, come in." He turns away from his monitor, and his eyes are laser beams tracking my movement as I sit in the chair across from him.

"I've got to tell you something and I think you'll be...disappointed."

"Well, don't leave me in suspense. It's been a good two hours since someone has pissed me off. I don't want to wait any longer." His Cheshire Cat grin doesn't help.

"I didn't know it at the time, but my girlfriend, ex-girlfriend, was part of the Genloran study."

Bob shakes his head like he's trying to clear away gnats. "That girl, Gina? She's crazy?"

"No, not crazy. She's autistic, or was. I don't know." My nerves thrust me out of the chair, and I pace in front of Breckner's cartoonishly large desk. "When I first met her, I had no idea she was on any medication. She never even mentioned it, not until long after we started buying Genloran."

Bob rummages through his top drawer, finds a couple of antacids, and chews with a force that might dislodge his veneers.

I wait for him to respond, but all he does is tap his fingers on the highly polished cherry wood.

"I swear. I know it sounds lame, but it's true." I continue to pace, because looking at Breckner only makes me tenser.

"Okay. Let's think this through. There's no reason this needs to leave this room. And if it comes down to it, I'm assuming Gina will sign an affidavit stating she had not disclosed her participation in the study to you until a date well after we started buying."

"Yeah…" I stop in front of the window, because I am not going to look him in the eye when I drop the next bomb. "We sort of broke up, and she's about to do a media interview about her experience."

The silence is broken by a crackling. I turn and see that he has snapped his keyboard in half.

"Take the rest of the day off." His voice is deadly calm. "It's best if you're out of the building while we make an action plan."

I formulate a protest, but he doesn't look at me. He merely picks up his phone and places a call.

I trudge down the hall and step into my office to grab my coat. How much longer will it be my office?

I wave to Rob on my way out, but it's best for him if we don't speak, so I ignore his beckoning gesture. I barely glance at the security guard to say good-bye.

New York in early spring is damp, dreary, and

chilly. The joy of winter is gone and it's not warm enough to enjoy walking outdoors.

But I plan to walk uptown to my apartment. At two in the afternoon, there's not much else to do.

I take out my phone and pull up Gina's number. She asked that I not call her, and my head says to obey her wishes. The rest of my being says there is no one else who can see me through this.

I see three missed calls. Two are from Marco and one from my mother.

Listening to the voice messages seems like too much effort. So I return Marco's call.

"Chris, where the hell have you been?" There's a strain in his voice and shouting in the background.

"I'm at work and couldn't get to my phone. What's going on?"

"Come home. Pop is missing."

I hang up without asking another question. I hail a cab and throw some bills at the driver when he protests about hauling out to Queens.

The ride goes by in a blur, and not just because I'm too freaked out to focus on anything. An icy rain pelts down, and as we emerge from the tunnel, it's a torrent. The cab's wipers, turned on high, barely make a visible field for the driver. He curses in his native language and arrives at the corner to my home.

"This street is a mess. I can't get down there."

"Fine," I bark. But I see what he means. It's not

just the puddles becoming lakes—two police cars have blocked the way.

I yank open the car door and slosh down the block.

Momma stands in the doorway, a scarf over her head, and she wrings her hands. She speaks to a police officer who is taking notes, and her face is pinched.

"Chris." Marco jogs over to me, water running down his raincoat. He motions for me to join him in his car.

I slide into the front seat, bringing a puddle of water with me.

"What happened?"

He rubs his hands together and cranks up the heat. "Pop was on the back porch. Momma was folding laundry. She went to check on him, and he was gone. That was two hours ago."

"Shit."

Through the windshield Momma turns away from the officer and allows Maria to bring her inside.

"I was walking up and down the streets. But now I think I'll drive. Want to come with me?"

"Yeah, but wait while I let Momma know I'm here."

Opening the door lets in even more water.

Dashing to the house doesn't make a difference. I'm already soaked.

"Momma?" I call as I enter.

"Christofo." She says my name as softly as she did when I was sick with pneumonia.

I kneel in front of her and take her hands. "We'll find him. Marco and I will drive around."

"The police are looking, too," Maria says, and rubs Momma's shoulder.

My mother has shrunk over the years. She was never a big woman, but her presence made her tower above us.

"I only left him alone for a little while. He's never been gone this long."

"He's left before?"

"If you came around here instead of spending time with that crazy girl, you'd know the problems we deal with."

"Gina is not crazy, and I've been here plenty of times for you to let me know that my father wanders off. I though you all said he couldn't get out of the yard, Momma." I stand and challenge her with my glare to scold me for getting the carpet wet. "This can't go on. Pop needs to be somewhere safe." Despite the chill from the rain seeping down my neck, I burn with anger. "I've said this before. Gina was the one who told us he needs to be somewhere safe. A place that can care for him."

"And you'd visit him? Or would you let him rot in some home, ignoring him like you ignore the rest of your family? Will you abandon us again, Christofo? Like last time?"

"I guess I deserve that. But you never make it easy, Momma." I kick the hassock out of the way in my haste to the door. "I'm going out with Marco to look for him. But this conversation isn't over. You need to forgive me for what I did when I was a kid, and I promise to forgive you for being so hard to love."

I exit to the front step when a police cruiser pulls up. The officer approaches the house.

"Mr. Rinaldi?"

"I'm one of them."

"We found your father. He's at Memorial. We took him there because he was in bad shape. Cold and confused."

I jump back into the house. "He's at the hospital," I call to Momma.

She's on her feet and grabbing her purse before I can thank the police officer.

Chapter 24

GINA

My phone chimes a text again. I see something about Chris's father, but I delete it before I get sucked into something with him. I told Chris not to contact me until I figure things out, but even in this, he needs to work an angle, put in his two cents. I run through as many idioms as I can think of, because maybe I will lose the ability to understand the subtleties of speech. Maybe once again, I'll be left to the fringes of conversations.

In any case, I don't answer his text. He doesn't get to decide what happens. For as long as possible, I will set my own boundaries.

Jennifer walks in and drops into her chair.

"Gina, I'm so glad you're here. How are you doing?"

"I'm studying every clue on your face. Your furrowed brow, your down-turned mouth. The way you lean forward toward me. Your eyes searching my face for a sign as to whether I'm okay."

"Gina." Jennifer's eyes well up. "If I had known…"

I shake my head. "I still would have gone through with it. I think."

She takes my hand, and the kindness seeps through her palm into mine. I grasp it and allow the tears to splash onto the floor.

"I don't even mind feeling sad now." I gulp air. "I feel something."

Jennifer leans farther forward and holds me.

"You've been through so much this past year." She pats my back, and I calm down.

When we straighten ourselves, she hands me a box of tissues.

"We have a lot to figure out." I pull out a list I made. "I have to write things down. I think I'm beginning to lose some memory." I let the paper fall into my lap. "No, I remember everything that happens. I just don't remember to plan for things. Yesterday, I knew I had plans to go out with Franny, but I forgot that I would want to wear something different for going out, so I kept my ratty jeans and old sweatshirt on. When we met at the club she looked at me but didn't say anything. I didn't fit in. Again."

"Maybe this list is a good idea. When you get those emotional cues, write them down." Jennifer peers at the paper.

"I need to talk about relationships. That's this first item."

"All relationships?"

"No, just with Chris. Or with another boy. Should I still have romantic relationships? Should someone like me have sex? Is that a ridiculous question?" The laugh gets lodged in my throat.

"No. I think you proved me and your grandmother wrong. You forged a real intimate and meaningful bond with Chris. Does he want to end it?"

"He keeps calling." I shake my phone. "But I don't want to doom him to a life with me. As I was. Or I don't know how I'll cope when he breaks up with me. Maybe I should stick with my career. That's the one thing that doesn't seem to be slipping away. My thoughts are crystal clear in school. I'm getting A's in my classes and got an internship at a furniture design shop."

"Gina, that's fabulous. There are many people who'd give up a lot to be successful in a career."

"Would they give up love?"

"Do you think you'll stop loving?"

"It hurts so much to be away from him. At least that lets me know I'm still in love. Even if I can't quite think of a way to show him now." I huff. "There's no answer for that now. Can we move on to item number two?"

"Sure. What's next on Gina's emotional to-do list?" Jennifer smiles, and I cling to the idea that she is joking. I know it's a good kind of joke, one that is meant to draw us close.

I return the smile with ease, and relax. It's all still there, it just takes a few more seconds to access.

"The interview about the drug companies." I flutter my hands and clasp them together. "If I do it, I might not have to make a decision about Chris. That might be the nail in the coffin of our relationship." One more idiom.

"Would he really be that upset?"

"He'd likely lose his job. And probably be unable to get another one. I won't mention him. But everyone at his work knows who I am. They'll know that I was taking the drug he was betting on. They'll assume we talked about it." I suck in a breath. "But aren't some things more important than individuals? Isn't it critical that people know what happened so that companies can't just get away with this?"

"That's a value judgment. I can't answer that. What are ways to check in with your beliefs, and see what's right for you? What's most important?"

I get up and pace her office. Counting each step so that I end in prime numbers before I turn around. Thirteen one direction, eleven the other.

"If I go back to the way I was before, I at least want my experience to have meant something. I want some record of how I was. I want it remembered that I was normal. That I loved and was loved, and that I lost it all." I stop on step number eight and fight against the itch on my back. "Is that selfish? To do it for those reasons? To care more about telling my story than about how it might help others?"

"No." Jennifer runs her hand over her head. "All of us need some validation, and you have an opportunity to get it on a grand scale. And like you said, it might be your only opportunity."

And if I lose Chris, I lose him. I'll either be able to have a relationship or not. There are plenty of fish in the sea. One more figure of speech I try to cement in my brain. Even though I know it's not true.

CHRIS

I never listen to NPR. Bloomberg usually has all the information I need. So it takes me a minute to find the station. I slip my earbuds in, and Gina's voice fills my head.

The words don't register at first. It's natural to have her breathy cadence so close to my brain. I need to shake myself. Everyone can hear her, not just me. Everyone.

"I can clearly remember signing the consent forms. And I had read it carefully," Gina says.

"And was there anything in the forms about how the drug trial would end?" The reporter's voice is clipped and efficient.

I pull my small collection of books off the shelf and bang them into one of the boxes security provided for me. I have to be ready to go in twenty minutes, when I'll be escorted from the building. The security guard is doing his best to seem casual outside my office door. But his occasional glance inside lets me know he is making sure I'm taking only what's mine.

There isn't anything else to take. The slightly askew pictures and out-of-order files show me that someone has gone through my desk, and also removed my computer before I arrived.

My Little League trophy has collected some dust. I wipe it clean.

"When I was taking the drug regularly, I felt so different. It's hard to explain to someone who hasn't had the experience. You come out of a fog, from a place where you only get about half of the information. Like learning a new language in a foreign country. At first, you understand just the basics. 'Hello.' 'How much does this cost?'" There's a familiar catch in her voice, and I can visualize what her face looks like at that moment. Her brow is pinched and her nose is crinkled. "Then you become more fluent, and one day you're speaking like a native. But there was always a part of me who felt out of place, like I was just pretending."

"But you did accomplish so much. You're enrolled in a design program, and you have an internship."

"Yes, but I think I could have always done those things. I just lacked the confidence or even the awareness to pursue those. It was the friendships, the relationships, that I could have never formed."

"Tell me about those. Do you still have those connections?"

"Well." The lengthy pause rips my chest open. The pain in that one word smacks against my eardrum, and doubles me over as if I've been punched. "I do and I don't." Gina's sigh tells me she has collected herself, but the tremble in her speech remains. "I have to think about it more consciously. I have to run through steps in my head, decode the language. It's not as natural as it was before. But yes. I still get along with my friends, and they have all been very supportive."

"And will it remain? Will you still be able to run through the steps? Because sitting with you here, I can't tell that you aren't picking up on any social cues."

She laughs, and it's the kind of laugh that would have tickled my hair if she were as close to me as my earbuds are.

"I'm paying very close attention to your eyes," Gina says. "They can tell me a lot about if someone is trying to be sarcastic, and when someone is waiting for a response."

I sink into my chair, and for the last time gaze out my window onto the bustling street below. Everyone snatching at opportunities, rolling the dice. Some will come up with boxcars, some snake eyes.

"Mr. Rinaldi, we need to get going." The

security guard sticks his head in and motions for me to follow him.

I nod and heft the box under my arm, but keep listening as we proceed to the elevator bank.

Appearing as if I'm engaged in music is easier than saying good-bye. Rob tries to catch my attention. But it's best for both of us if he's not seen talking with me.

I focus back on the interview.

"What do you have to say to Genloran?" the reporter asks.

"I don't think I have anything to say. It's not fair, but it is what I signed on for. I wasn't mentally incompetent. I knew what I was signing. I was incompetent about understanding it, though. I knew all the words on the page. I knew that it said the trial would end, and I may not benefit. But I had no concept of how I would feel about it. And anyway, it may not have been the drug. Who knows why I am the only person of the hundreds they tested to have made this progress."

The elevator dings, and I step on, followed by the guard. The doors swoosh closed and my chest expands with a breath. Straps that have kept me bound tightly over the past few years loosen. Those straps also gave me a direction.

I lose the signal in the elevator but keep my eyes glued to the numbers counting down to the lobby. The doors open and light from the atrium hits my face.

"I don't know," Gina says in response to some question I missed. "I'm hoping that I'm done losing my skills. Feeling emotions is so powerful. It can be overwhelming, uncomfortable, and even devastating. But for anyone who feels any kind of grief, you should know it's so much better than not feeling anything."

The guard nods to me as I push through the revolving door. The sun shines, but it's cold. I still need my coat, which I left at home, thinking my anger would keep me warm.

Is it better to feel grief than not feel anything? Right now I'd go for a bit of autism.

Chapter 25

GINA

"And from the photos you showed me, I think this fabric would contrast best with that blue wall." I hold the swatch out to the woman who reminds me of Breckner's wife. I wouldn't be surprised if I met one of the women at a Humbolt and Sutter party. The memory of Chris's hand on the small of my back makes my mouth go dry.

"I'm just not sure." She weighs two other swatches in her hands, and fingers them. Her mouth turns down, and she's not unhappy. Just unsure.

My job is to help her feel sure. Offer advice and information.

"This one" — I touch the one in her left hand — "is less expensive and won't show stains. This other one has a softer feel and might give out sooner. But the color is closer to what you're looking for."

"You're the expert." She shrugs a perfectly tan shoulder. "Let's go with the more luxurious one. If I don't like it, I can always have it reupholstered." She flounces to the counter, where the manager will add up her bill.

I trail behind with the swatch.

I read her perfectly. She only wanted someone to validate what she was already thinking. She didn't need advice. She needed agreement. A reason to buy the pricier one.

The balloon in my chest inflates just a little. It's exhausting, but with the extra effort I can keep up with decoding the emotions.

"We'll need about ten yards, plus the foam..." The manager taps at her calculator.

"Six hundred and thirty-two dollars," I say without even thinking.

Both faces turn toward me. "I think." I feel my face flush, and back away.

They mumble to each other, and I try to etch a reminder in my mind not to do that anymore. It freaks people out.

The front door opens, and Sarah waves frantically to get my attention.

"I'm going on my lunch break," I say to the manager, and grab my bag.

Sarah gives me a thumbs-up as I approach.

"Wow, look at you." She barely keeps her voice to a whisper, and a few heads turn our way. At least I remember what it feels like to be embarrassed.

I take her elbow and we're outside. March is damp and rattling cold. I didn't grab my coat because I get forty-five minutes for lunch and didn't want to waste time going to the back.

"That place is so high end. I had no idea you'd

made it to the big time."

"I'm the intern. I work for practically nothing while they rake it in on customers with more money than sense."

"I heard your interview." Sarah squeezes my arm, and we enter the falafel shop.

It's crowded and steamy in the narrow passage between the counter and the wall. People push forward to place orders.

"Hey there, Gina." Manny, the Latino owner of the Middle Eastern food stall, winks at me from his place at the grill. "The table is for you and your friend." He shouts something in Spanish to an Asian guy, who places a small café table and two rickety wooden chairs at the back.

"Whoa." Sarah slides into the seat. "You're some kind of celebrity here?"

"That's me. Queen of the falafel hut." I smile because it is comical how Manny fawns over me. "He wants to set me up with his son."

"Is he cute?" Sarah's eyes widen when one of the workers places baskets of pita overflowing with falafel, tahini, and cucumbers on the table.

"Yes. But I'm not interested now."

"Uh-oh." Sarah lets the oozing sandwich drop into the red plastic basket. "Are you not interested, not interested, or just not interested?"

I close my eyes and try to parse this out. "Sarah, I'm too tired. Does that even mean something to someone without autism?"

"Sorry, that was vague. I meant, are you not interested because you don't want to date the falafel king's son, or are you not interested because you've...you know...become uninterested?" She eyes me up and down, as if my autism might pop out of my gut like an alien.

"No, I still like boys." I dig into my food because I'm starved and because I don't want to linger in the back of the overflowing shop. "I really miss sex. If you must know." And Chris, but I can't say that aloud.

"Oh thank God." Sarah picks up her pita again. "I thought you'd slid back into that shell." She takes a bite and moans. "But please reconsider the falafel guy. This is amazing. You could give up sex for this."

"Sarah, was I really that bad? Did I really come across as cold and distant as I remember?"

She swallows and swallows again. I've made her uncomfortable. But I need this information.

"You were so hard to talk to. Never mean, never difficult to get along with. But not much fun." She turns away. "Do you hate me for saying that?"

"No, I think I love you for it." The fried chickpeas form a mass in my stomach, and I push the basket away.

"I'll stick by you no matter what. But you'd better not come back to work at the coffee shop. You'd better become the best interior designer around."

"I will." A smile pulls at my lips, and it's so nice for the natural response to be there. "It comes easier when I'm relaxed. When I'm nervous or lose my confidence, all my abilities to read people rush out the window. Rush out the window. A metaphor."

"Yeah, it is. But don't say so aloud."

"Right." I nod. Gotta keep some thoughts to myself, even if they are correct.

"Any word from Chris?"

"No. I told him not to call, and he stopped. I suppose he lost his job because of my interview."

"You don't feel guilty about that, do you?"

"Yes, I do. But maybe it was best to finally end things. He can't still want to be with me after that. I'm sad for him. Really, because that's what he always wanted. A place outside of Queens, money, and power. I hope he finds another way to achieve that."

"And there's no chance you'll get back with him?"

"I can't see a way past this. He has lost what he thought was all he had to offer. I'm struggling to maintain. I could never be the partner he needs in the kind of life he wants."

"You don't believe that." Sarah licks her fingers and sits back. "You have enough emotions left for them to get all fuddled up. That much I can see."

"Well, at least that's something."

CHRIS

There's a hum of activity but mostly a peaceful atmosphere in the day room. Soft music comes from unseen speakers.

Most residents sit around tables and read magazines. A few are watching TV. Pop shuffles a deck of cards and lays them out for a game of solitaire.

"He's doing quite well." The social worker guides me inside.

"I haven't seen him do anything other than sit in front of the television in a long time." I hover near his table. "I don't want to disturb him."

"Join him." She pulls the chair next to him out for me, and steps away.

"Hi, Pop." I sit and try to make eye contact, but he's intent on his game. "I heard you're doing well. Do you like it here?"

"I need a black eight." He points to a red nine. His knuckles stretch the pale skin, but his nails are clipped and cleaner than I've ever seen them. A man who worked for the sanitation department always had cuts on his hands and scraggly nails.

"Yeah. Maybe one will come up." I tap the pile of cards.

He flips through a few times and then looks at me. "Joe?"

"No, it's me, Chris." I pat his arm, and he watches as if it's not his own arm. Surprised that he can feel the sensation of someone else.

He goes back to his game.

"I'm living somewhere else, too," I continue. No one is listening, so I might as well unburden myself. "I got a place in Brooklyn. Not Italian Brooklyn or Jewish Brooklyn — Hipster Brooklyn. All I can afford now. I got fired. Made a stupid decision and, well, I lost the gamble. Maybe it wasn't for me anyway. Maybe I should choose a different career. Not sure who will hire me at this point."

"Joe lost his job at the navy yard." Pop squints at the cards and shakes his head.

"Here, put this two up on the ace," I offer.

He nods. "He was fighting with one of the other boys. The brother of that girl. First, his dick gets him into trouble, then his fists."

I laugh. "He's not the only one. I lost my girl, too. That's even worse. I can find another job, probably. But another girl? Well, not one like that. Do you remember Regina Giancarlo?"

"The slow girl down the street. She loves Carina. They play together. She watches out for Carina. The rest of you are too old to play with her. Carina. Our little *princessa*. She needs a playmate. Gina is a good playmate. She's slow, but has a good heart, loves everyone, never a bad word. Not like that mother of hers. Evil woman, doesn't know what an angel of a daughter she has."

"Yeah. She's an angel. She's not appreciated."

"Christofo, you're here." Momma enters, followed by Marco.

"I said I would be." I stand and hug her and punch my brother in the arm.

"Pop looks great," I say.

Momma's lips purse, but she gives a tight nod. "They take care of him. He does more now."

"You should see him in dance class," Marco says. "They play the piano, and all the old folks move around to the music. Pop gets into it."

"Of course. He always loved to dance," Momma spits out, as if Marco is dim-witted for being surprised.

"We should get going. I'll get his coat." Marco walks down to Pop's room, and Momma and I watch the next game of solitaire begin.

"He'll like going to church. He always likes services during Lent." Momma pushes his hair from his face. "They should get his hair cut. He likes his hair short."

"Maria told me you're volunteering at Saint John's school."

Momma shrugs and watches the hallway for Marco. "I have so much time on my hands. What am I supposed to do? Besides, that school needs all the hands they can get with the kids from Our Lady of Peace combining in there." Her mouth is set in a firm line, but her chin juts out, and I can tell she's proud and happy to be engaged in something she feels passionate about. "What about you? You have a new job?"

"Not yet. I don't even know where to start."

She snorts. "All that education, and you don't know how to get a job. How are you going to pay your bills?"

"They gave me a big severance package." I continue to answer the confusion on her face. "Technically, I resigned, and they gave me a chunk of money so I wouldn't cause any trouble."

"And you plan to live off this chunk? For how long? Seems as though you know how to invest money. Why don't you tell people how to invest money?"

"It's not like that. I'm not a stockbroker. I analyze the market—"

Her raised eyebrow cuts me off.

Marco returns with the coat. "Come on. I parked out in front."

Pop protests a bit about leaving his card game, but acquiesces when we help him into his coat.

"I could use some fresh air. This break room is too stuffy." Pop rises from his seat and scans the room. "All the boys coming back from their shift."

Momma rolls her eyes and takes Pop's arm. Marco and I follow them.

"Thanks for driving us all to church," I say.

"No problem. Driving, that's what I do."

"Marco, you've got a family, kids. You've got what's important. Look at me. I had more money and power than was good for me. Poof, it's gone. I've got to start from scratch."

"What about Gina?"

"She's done with me. She was too upset about losing the medication. It's for the best."

"Really?"

"No, it's the worst. But what future did we have together? Especially now that I have nothing to offer."

"I can't believe she was only interested in your money. Anyway, didn't I hear you have a big wad of it now? How long will it last you?"

"A long time. I sold my condo in Manhattan. A pile of money just sitting there."

"There's a lot you can do with a load of cash." Marco unlocks his car, and we scoot Pop in the front seat. Momma and I sit in back.

"Your backseat is tiny," she complains. "Is this going to be every Sunday?"

"Until I get a bigger car or you learn to fly," Marco grumbles under his breath. But not low enough. Momma cuffs him on the back of the head, and we head off to Saint John's Church to celebrate the peace of the Lenten season.

GINA

Nonna and I wedge into the church. The place is packed with the regulars and all the people who come just at Easter. Lilies decorate the altar, and the hum of voices drowns out the organ music. The pews are especially crowded because today is the first Easter the parishioners from Our Lady of Peace are joining Saint John's. Services during Lent were so crowded, Nonna and I had to stand in the back, and we were swept out at the end. She insisted we get there early this time, but finding a seat was still tough.

"Where are we supposed to sit?" Nonna clasps my elbow so we stick together.

"I see Aunt Sophie over there. She must have saved some seats." I cram through the bodies, and sure enough, there is just enough space for Nonna and me to squish in.

Nonna chats with her sister, and I finger the edge of the bulletin. It welcomes the new members and talks about how the schools have merged successfully. I read it because I don't want to talk to the scattering of familiar people who smile, make eye contact, and expect me to hold up half of a conversation.

Everyone has gotten used to the social Gina. The Gina who can tell jokes, and understand jokes. The Gina who smiles easily and has fun.

That Gina is still inside me. I want to smile and have fun. I want to share jokes. It just takes a little more effort than it did when I had the drug.

"Gina, tell us about college." Aunt Sophie leans over.

I resist the urge to list my courses and assignments. Instead I dig deep.

"I'm very interested in the design workshop, where we are paired with nonprofits to design a space. I'm working at the Autism Center. They desperately need some work done."

"Oh." Aunt Sophie's voice pierces the air.

I smile easily. Her discomfort shouldn't be funny, but it is.

"Gina has so much to give back to the center."

"But didn't they..." Aunt Sophie's face pinches tightly.

"Yes, I'm out of the medicine now. Have been for over a month." I hold my hands out. "But I'm hanging in there." I use an idiom and maintain eye contact.

Aunt Sophie and Nonna return to safer subjects, and I cast my gaze around the room. Even more people have come in. The air is thick, and the noise level increases. I close my eyes and take a few deep breaths.

I need a nap. I still have all the skills and can call them up whenever I want. I just don't want to very often.

Eventually, the priest emerges and mass begins. The familiarity and routine comforts me.

A year ago, I also would have been comforted by mass, but in a different way. Before I had my skills, I needed the routine to quiet my agitation. Now, the routine gives me an outlet for my mind to explore the depths of who I am.

I was never cured of autism. I don't think it's something to cure. Without it, I could never visualize a design, manage our stock portfolio, or have my unique perspective on human emotions.

But now, I can leverage it better. Bring it out when I need to and wield it like a sword against mediocrity.

And if I get up the energy, I can connect with people in ways I never could before. Experience intimacy. I suspect many people without autism never have the kind of relationship I had with Chris. Or even the loving friendships I have with Sarah and Franny. Just because you lack autism doesn't mean you automatically have good relationships.

We file out into the center aisle to receive communion. The people on the opposite side do the same. Two parallel lines inch forward.

"Gina." My name is a whisper, drifting to me from the left.

Chris Rinaldi stands next to me. Our shoulders inches apart.

"Chris." I hear a plea in my voice.

"I've missed you." His hand brushes mine, like he's going to take hold of it then thinks better of it.

"Me too." I try to swallow past the sandpaper sensation in my throat. "What happened at work?"

He gives a bitter laugh. "I was asked to resign. But I got a huge payout and just started a new job."

"Another financial firm?" We proceed sedately down the aisle side by side.

"Don't think I'll find anyone willing to take me on Wall Street. I'm working for a small firm that invests money from nonprofits in companies with good social practices. Places that pay above minimum wage, offer employee ownership, use green energy."

"Shhh," Nonna hisses from behind me.

Chris and I rub arms as we walk. I almost slip my arm through his as we pass another row of pews. With Chris, I don't have to think as hard about the skills. My responses to him have been laid down in my neural pathways. There's no way to erase them.

The line stops moving, and for a moment, the music quiets and I can hear the sound of my heartbeat. Chris and I watch each other.

"Sounds like it doesn't pay much." I discover a wry smile tugging at my lips. My emotions come so easily with Chris. It's a drenching relief of cool water on a hot day to react so automatically.

"Nope, just enough to keep me in off-the-rack suits and my studio in Brooklyn."

"A fall from grace?"

"Maybe I've found a different grace. I can see you're doing well." His eyes plead with me for a connection.

"How can you tell? Sorry. I didn't mean that to sound like an accusation."

"I know you didn't. I know you're simply curious as to how I can see you've still got a handle on the emotional world." He turns his head from the line ahead and looks into my eyes. "You still have the light in your eyes. You still have that smile and the gentle tilt of your head."

I gasp. Warmth runs down my spine. A good warmth, not the overheated itch from the press of bodies.

"Hush," Mrs. Rinaldi snaps directly behind Chris.

The music plays on as the communion bowl is replenished with more wafers.

The altar comes into view and only a few people are ahead of us.

"I can't tell you how good it is to see you." His voice is a homecoming, settling the disquiet that wouldn't budge for weeks.

I'm in front. As the priest recites the words and I open my mouth, Chris whispers, "I always knew I'd walk down the aisle with you."

I laugh and find a communion wafer thrust inside. I nearly choke while trying to stifle my giggles.

I get the stink eye from the priest for my inappropriate response.

"Sorry," I sputter. "I'm autistic."

Chris chuckles and returns to his seat with his family.

The rest of the service passes by in a blur. I sneak glances at Chris, and he winks at me every time our eyes meet. The balloon that had deflated in my chest swells again. I don't have to think about smiling.

Nonna pats my arm, and when I look at her, her eyes are filled with tears.

"Go to him. He's good for you." Her mouth is by my ear and I smell her lavender soap.

The recessional hymn plays, and it seems to take hours for Chris and me to meet in the aisle.

"Christofo, help me, please." A hoarse whisper comes from behind Chris.

I twist and see Mrs. Rinaldi grasping Mr. Rinaldi by the elbow, struggling to keep him shuffling along with the rest of us.

"Here, Pop." Chris takes his father's other arm, and we're four abreast as we come to a standstill.

"Mrs. Rinaldi, happy Easter. And a happy Easter to you, Mr. Rinaldi."

"Gina, you're looking well." Mrs. Rinaldi nods, and her husband smiles.

"It's great your dad can come."

"What do you think? That Chris would leave his

father in a nursing home for Easter?" Mrs. Rinaldi purses her lips and the line moves forward a bit. "He's arranged transportation every Sunday for anyone from Our Lady of Peace parish who needs a ride here. He pays for the shuttle bus himself."

"You raised a good boy, Rose." Nonna's voice from behind me is carefree, as if she and Mrs. Rinaldi are old friends meeting at the salon for a perm.

"And Gina is a good girl. Bright, very bright. Happy Easter, Catherine."

Nonna thanks her, and we all inch forward as the crowd tries to exit. "My Gina looks very happy today. Happier than she's been in a while." Her fingers poke into my back.

She's right. The effortless smile has stretched my cheeks.

"I am happy to see you." I turn to him, and his charming smile infects me. It fires all those pathways and sends my thoughts away from the solemnity of the occasion.

And I find that he has taken my hand. With one arm propping up his father and his other entwined with mine, he brings his face down to my ear.

"I've wanted to hear you say that for so long." His breath moves my hair out of place, but moves my heart back to where it's supposed to be.

"Catherine, you'll ride back with me in the shuttle bus. You and Gina are coming over for Easter dinner." Mrs. Rinaldi smiles, probably the first smile

I've ever seen from her.

"Rose, that would be very nice."

My mouth hangs open, and I stare at Chris.

"I guess that leaves you and me to take a cab." Chris's hand moves from clasping mine to resting on the small of my back, and brings me to the time when intimacy with him was an everyday thing.

He breaks contact to help his father down the steps and into the coach.

"Nonna, is this okay?" I need her to voice it aloud. I need to hear someone echo the reality in my head. I don't trust my autistic brain to make this decision right here on the steps of the church.

"Who am I to say what's okay?" She follows Mrs. Rinaldi onto the bus.

Chris stands with me as we watch them drive off.

"Where's the rice?" He scans the crowd and furrows his brow.

"Rice?"

"It's traditional to throw rice at the bride and groom as they exit the church." His eyes search my face, but there's that mischievous grin and heavy-lidded eyes.

A current of doubt courses from me, as I know for sure what will make me happy. I slip my hand around his waist. His body presses into my side.

"Christopher Rinaldi, I don't remember you asking me to marry you."

"That's because you never gave me the chance." He lowers his face, and his lips are so close I could kiss him, but I pull back.

"Well, here's your chance." I cross my arms over my chest and grin.

A flash of panic widens his eyes, but he recovers.

"Wait here. Don't move." He dashes into the swarm of people mingling after the service. He's jumping up, searching over people's heads. He calls something and makes a direct path through the throng to a guy in a black windbreaker.

They bend their heads together and seem to argue for a moment. Chris reaches into his pocket and hands the guy a wad of bills.

Chris turns and scoots around families to come back to me.

"Who was that?"

"Some guy who buys stuff."

"Looks like he was selling stuff."

"I was just getting back what was mine. But I hope it will be yours." He opens his hand, and the same diamond ring he presented to me weeks ago is nestled in his palm. "I finally sold it this morning. I had given up hope. But you're here."

"Do you really want me? Like I am?"

"Gina." He kneels down and takes my hand. Heads have turned and the conversations fade. All the cell phones are trained on us. "I wouldn't want you any other way. The question is, do you want me?

The way I am now, a new man. I've got a purpose and a direction. No money, but a newfound confidence. All because of who you are."

Hot tears ripple down my cheeks. I nod. Because I think if I open my mouth, I'll scream with joy. And screaming doesn't seem right. So I nod some more.

"Oh no. If you made me get down on my knee to ask, then, Gina Giancarlo, you'd better say the words." His eyes slant and the corners of his mouth turn up.

"Yes, Christopher Rinaldi." My voice is too loud, I can tell. But I don't care. "Please put that ring on my finger. And I will marry you."

"Ha!" He slides the ring on and leaps up.

My feet leave the ground as he twirls me, and I do scream. Probably most women would cheer in a feminine way, but I scream.

When my feet come down to earth, Chris's lips come down over mine. The kiss brings me back to all our kisses. The kisses in the back of taxis, the kisses in my room, the kisses in his apartment. The kiss New Year's Eve when I silently begged him not to propose because I was scared.

And all those kisses have blazed a path in my heart and my mind.

And now this kiss hums in my bones and is for the future.

When we break apart, I hear the applause and feel heat creep to my face.

"Let's get out of here." Chris drapes his arm across my shoulder, and I fit into the space that I carved out months ago.

"Should we go to your family's house?" I don't really want to, but part of me can't wait to show Nonna my hand. The ring will take some getting used to, as the metal digs a bit into my finger, and the weight is distracting. Women without autism probably delight in the sensation.

"We'll join them, eventually." He kisses the top of my head as we wind our way to the corner. "I want you to myself for a little while."

"Christopher Rinaldi, can I get you a cup of coffee?" I look up into the face that I'll look up into until I can't look up anymore.

"Yes, but only because you know exactly how I take it."

THE END

Dear Readers,

I hope Chris and Gina stay with you for a while. They are both brave people who have faced their demons and I feel confident that whatever they face in the future, they'll overcome it together.

I've got some other books that feature non-typical romantic heroes and heroines. Check out my website (kateforestbooks.com) or sign up for my infrequent but amusing newsletter.

And don't forget to turn to the end of the book to read about my other brave couples.

Wishing You a Happy Ever After,
Kate

ACKNOWLEDGMENTS

I cannot publish this book without thanking the many people on my team that got me here. First off, my critique gals, Veronica Forand, Susan Scott Shelley, Lauren Strauss, Kate Lutter, and Maria Imbalzano. Writing is hardly a solitary process.

To Amy Sieberer and Caroline Bradley for being brave parents of kids on the spectrum and giving me such invaluable feedback.

Arielle Eckstut and David Sterry, the Book Doctors, for all their advice and guidance.

I need to thank my parents and my sister, Andrea Pyros, the real writer of the family, for not laughing at me when I said I was going to write a book.

My kids who learned to not interrupt, even when it looked like all I was doing was playing on the computer.

And a special thanks to my hero, Tom, the most patient husband in the world. No, the laundry still isn't folded.

ABOUT KATE FOREST

Author Kate Forest has worked in a psychiatric hospital, as a dating coach, and spent a disastrous summer selling aboveground swimming pools. But it was her over 20 year career as a social worker that compelled her to write love stories with characters you don't typically get to read about. She lives in Philadelphia with her husband, two kids, and a fierce corgi.

You can find her at:
http://www.KateForestBooks.com
Twitter: @KateForestBooks
Facebook:
https://www.facebook.com/KateForestAuthor

STANDING UP

Standing up for yourself doesn't require legs.

Brilliant physics major Jill Kramer tutors jocks in math to pay her tuition. The college junior has big dreams — NASA. And if her self-centered ex taught her anything, it's to never again let a guy distract her from her goals, especially the hottie failing calculus.

Former football star Mike Lewis hopes the cute calculus tutor will save his otherwise perfect GPA. Top grades will convince his demanding father that he's still pursuing law school and not his real dream — the Broadway stage. Acting seems unachievable at the moment, with him hunched over crutches and in crippling pain from a past car accident, but after amputation surgery he'll strut on state-of-the-art prosthetics.

Jill can't help but fall for Mike — brains in his head, muscles in his chest, and vulnerability in his legs. Mike loves her determination and her refusal to pity him.

But when choices have to be made — family versus goals, dreams versus love — they both need to find strength to stand on their own, side-by-side.

IN TUNE OUT OF SYNC

No one wants to play second fiddle in love.

Veronica "Ronnie" Lukas has one dream: playing violin with the New York Philharmonic. She'll do whatever she can to hide her dyslexia and inability to read music, because nothing, not even sexy and talented Scott Grossman, will stand in her way.

Since he first tucked a violin under his chin, Scott's tics caused by Tourette's Syndrome quieted. His talent has thrust him into the harsh spotlight, becoming a reluctant poster child for living with Tourette's.

When Scott wins first chair of a small regional orchestra, Ronnie begrudgingly accepts second. She wants to hate the humble man who is disarmingly open about his disability. Instead, she falls for his heavenly music — and toe-curling kisses. Despite keeping her dyslexia a secret, Scott is smitten with the brilliant woman who doesn't treat him with kid gloves.

There's only one spot open in the New York Philharmonic, but Scott and Ronnie find it's not the competition but their differing views that come to a crescendo — secrets versus truth, spotlight versus shadows. Finding their rhythm is tough when they're marching to their own beat.

Coming Oct 2017

89792008R00188

Made in the USA
Columbia, SC
25 February 2018